Lucien felt his mind and body ~~~~~ turbulent emotions that he'd held back for the past eighteen months

Now he was giving in to a hunger to a degree he hadn't known was possible. There was this ravenousness that was invading his body and obliterating any kind of control. And he was giving in to it. Letting it dominate.

Her tongue tasted just as he'd known it would, with a sweetness that was turning his cells into jelly. There was a faint taste of the spiced coffee she'd drank earlier, but mostly it was all woman and it was so captivating he couldn't imagine how it would be not to kiss her.

He pushed that thought out of his mind as he continued to devour her mouth, lips, tongue. There wasn't a part of her mouth he hadn't invaded and sampled to his heart's content. And she was kissing him back with a hunger just as greedy as his own.

Books by Brenda Jackson

Kimani Romance	Kimani Arabesque
	(all Madaris Family titles)
*Solid Soul	
*Night Heat	Tonight and Forever
*Beyond Temptation	A Valentine's Kiss
*Risky Pleasures	Whispered Promises
In Bed with Her Boss	Eternally Yours
*Irresistible Forces	One Special Moment
Just Deserts	Fire and Desire
The Object of His Protection	Something to Celebrate
Temperatures Rising	Secret Love
*Intimate Seduction	True Love
Bachelor Untamed	Surrender
*Hidden Pleasures	**Wrapped in Pleasure
Star of His Heart	**Ravished by Desire
Bachelor Unleashed	Sensual Confessions
In the Doctor's Bed	

*Steele Family titles
**Westmoreland Family titles

BRENDA JACKSON

is a die "heart" romantic who married her childhood sweetheart and still proudly wears the "going steady" ring he gave her when she was fifteen. Because she's always believed in the power of love, Brenda's stories always have happy endings. In her real-life love story, Brenda and Gerald, her husband of thirty-eight years, live in Jacksonville, Florida, and have two sons.

A *New York Times* bestselling author of over seventy-five romance titles, Brenda is a retiree from a major insurance company and now divides her time between family, writing and traveling with Gerald. You may write to Brenda at P.O. Box 28267, Jacksonville, Florida 32226, email her at WriterBJackson@aol.com or visit her website at www.brendajackson.net.

NEW YORK TIMES AND USA TODAY BESTSELLING AUTHOR

BRENDA JACKSON

IN THE DOCTOR'S BED

KIMANI
ROMANCE

To the love of my life, Gerald Jackson, Sr.
To all my readers. This one is for you.

Let love and faithfulness never leave you; bind them
around your neck, write them on the tablet of your heart.
—*Proverbs* 3:3

KIMANI PRESS™

**Recycling programs
for this product may
not exist in your area.**

ISBN-13: 978-0-373-86220-7

IN THE DOCTOR'S BED

Copyright © 2011 by Harlequin Books S.A.

www.kimanipress.com

Printed in U.S.A.

Dear Reader,

I enjoy doing continuity books where I get to work with other authors. In this particular continuity—Hopewell General Hospital—I got to work with three outstanding authors, Ann Christopher, Maureen Smith and Jacquelin Thomas.

The four of us are introducing you to the staff of Hopewell General and how interns face daily challenges, especially when it comes to love. I've always enjoyed a good medical show and admit to being a *General Hospital* fan. And being a romantic at heart, I love to read a sexy romance story with a sexy hero, and I believe these four stories will definitely satisfy any romantic cravings you might have.

I hope all of you enjoy reading Lucien and Jaclyn's story as much as I enjoyed writing it.

Happy reading!

Brenda Jackson

Chapter 1

The moment Jaclyn Campbell stepped off the elevator she felt her nerves kick in. Tension stirred in the pit of her stomach, and her pulse throbbed at the base of her throat. It was as if she was back in high school and had been called to the principal's office. The only difference was she wasn't sixteen anymore, but a twenty-six-year-old woman, an intern at Hopewell General Hospital, and she had gotten summoned to the office of the chief of staff, Dr. Germaine Dudley.

Taking a deep breath and inserting her sweaty hands in the pockets of her slacks, she paused at the desk of Dr. Dudley's administrative assistant, Mona Wells. The older woman glanced up from the paperwork just long enough to say, "Go on in, Dr. Campbell. They're waiting on you in the conference room."

They? The pit of Jaclyn's stomach nearly dropped to

the floor. Who were "they"? She wondered just what kind of trouble she had gotten into. Granted she and Kayla Tsang, E.R.'s head nurse, never saw eye-to-eye on much of anything. Jaclyn had known from the first day of orientation it would behoove her to stay out of the woman's way.

Nurse Tsang was a stickler for rules and had the attitude of an old sourpuss, which was sad for someone who was only thirty-five years old. Jaclyn smiled to herself upon recalling what her roommate and fellow intern, Isabelle Morales, had told her just last week. "Miss Thang"—as other staff members called the nurse behind her back—needed to get laid.

Quickly wiping the smile off her face and drawing in another deep breath, Jaclyn knocked on the door.

"Come in."

Jaclyn entered the room to find three individuals sitting at a long table. Her gaze first went to Dr. Dudley who was seated at the head of the table, and as usual his gaze raked over her. It wasn't the first time she'd thought the man had a roving eye. Isabelle also had caught him ogling her and other young female interns the same way. That was probably the only mark against the man. The married, sixty-something father of three was well-respected in the medical field, and he had some political clout as well because he and the governor were college chums.

Her gaze then swept across the length of the table. The woman seated to the right of Dr. Dudley was Camille Hunter, the attractive public relations director of the hospital. Although Jaclyn didn't know Camille that well, she'd always found the young woman friendly enough when they'd passed in the halls or met in the elevator.

And last but definitely not least was the man who'd captured Jaclyn's heart her first day at Hopewell. Dr. Lucien De Winter, chief resident.

She wasn't ashamed to admit to herself that she had a crush on the man and had for months. Her mother had warned her that it would be that way when she met her true mate. Jaclyn wasn't sure how Dr. De Winter would fit into her future, but right now he was just a nice specimen of a man that any woman would love to lay claim to.

Even while sitting down, Dr. De Winter was tall, and had a muscular build. His black hair was cropped short and he had the sexiest brown eyes any man had a right to have. And that neatly trimmed mustache and goatee only accentuated a pair of sensuous lips.

Their gazes met briefly before she swiftly moved her eyes back to Dr. Dudley. "Nurse Tsang said you wanted to see me, sir," she said.

"Yes, come in and join us, Dr. Campbell. We won't bite."

She nervously crossed the room and sat in one of the chairs that happened to be directly across from Dr. De Winter.

"Now, Dr. Campbell, the reason you were summoned here today was to first thank you for your bravery as well as your loyalty in reporting the drug abuse of one of your fellow interns. I know that wasn't an easy decision to make, and I want to assure you that you did the right thing and you are appreciated for doing so. We were hoping we would be able to handle this matter rather quietly, but it seems that won't be the case."

Jaclyn nodded, trying to follow what Dr. Dudley was saying, but her close proximity to Dr. De Winter was distracting her. Was that heat she felt radiating off the man? She wouldn't be surprised given how drawn she was to him. It was an attraction she'd constantly tried to downplay, thanks to the hospital's no-fraternization policy regarding managers and those reporting to them.

"The Matthews family has threatened the hospital with a lawsuit."

Jaclyn blinked. *Lawsuit?* That one word pulled her attention back to Dr. Dudley. "I don't understand, sir."

"And neither do we, Dr. Campbell. Thanks to you reporting to Dr. De Winter what you knew regarding Dr. Matthews and our own proof of certain events, we'd hoped the matter could be handled discreetly. However, we have been notified that the Matthews family has decided to sue the hospital."

Jaclyn raised a brow. "On what grounds?"

"That we reacted in the extreme and that Dr. Matthews was wrongfully terminated."

Jaclyn frowned. "How can they say that?" Although she'd asked the question, in a way she already knew the answer. The Matthewses just happened to be one of the richest families not only in Alexandria but in all of Virginia. It was a known fact they were Hopewell's biggest benefactors. They even had a wing named after them. Their son Terrence had also been an intern. Jaclyn hated being the reason for Terrence's termination, but she felt she'd done the right thing when she'd witnessed his attempting to steal drugs from the hospital pharmacy more than once.

"The hospital feels we had sufficient grounds to release him. And although we are faced with a lawsuit as well as the withdrawal of the Matthewses' support to the hospital, we will deal with it," Dr. Dudley said assuringly.

He then glanced over at Camille. "As public relations supervisor it will be your job, Ms. Hunter, to make sure the hospital maintains its stellar reputation through all of this. I can just imagine the type of image the Matthewses will try painting us with."

Camille nodded, her expression sober. "I will."

Dr. Dudley smiled at Camille, a smile that made Jaclyn's flesh crawl. She wondered if she was the only one who'd caught on to it. She glanced over at Dr. De Winter and their gazes met, and not for the first time she thought she felt something emitting from the dark eyes holding hers.

Knowing she was just imagining things, she drew in a deep breath and shifted her attention back to Dr. Dudley as a question suddenly burned in her mind. "Now that there's a lawsuit pending, does that mean I will be named as the person who was…"

"The whistle-blower?" Dr. Dudley finished for her. "You won't have that to worry about. Your name will be held in the strictest confidence and protected by hospital policy. It has been proven that Dr. Matthews does indeed have a drug problem and it will be up to the Matthews family to prove otherwise."

Jaclyn was glad to hear that. She knew that once the news broke everyone would wonder who had snitched on Terrence because he was well-liked and had a promising future. It hadn't taken her long to figure him out and she'd been able to read the signs mainly because her older brother had had the same problem before he'd gotten help. Now he was married with a little girl and volunteered a lot of his time trying to help others kick the habit that had nearly destroyed him eight years ago.

"And because of the sensitive nature of the matter and the Matthews family's association with this facility, we have decided to hire someone to handle the suit that is not one of our regular hospital attorneys. In other words, we've decided to bring in the big guns."

"But we can assure you again, Dr. Campbell, that your confidentiality won't be compromised," Dr. De Winter interjected.

Jaclyn nodded while trying to ignore the warm, husky tone of his voice that seemed to caress every inch of her skin. She glanced over at him, met his gaze, felt her heart rate quicken. "Thank you."

"That will be all, Dr. Campbell," Dr. Dudley said, reclaiming her attention.

"All right." She stood and turned to leave. Although she was tempted to glance back over her shoulder to look at one person in particular, she was fully aware that doing so would be foolish as well as risky, so she continued to move toward the door.

Lucien entered his Georgetown row house at close to eight that night, hours later than his schedule at the hospital dictated. But then when was the last time he had what he considered a bona fide schedule? Certainly not since he'd taken the role of chief resident at Hopewell. At least this group of interns was halfway through this leg of their training. He had high hopes they would become good physicians one day. Some more so than others. There were a few he still needed to work on.

And one in particular he needed to keep his mind off.

Scowling, he paused and rubbed his hands down his face. Jaclyn Campbell would be his downfall if he wasn't careful. He of all people knew the hospital's nonfraternization policy and the consequences if it wasn't obeyed. Yet that hadn't stopped him from remembering every single thing about her whenever he saw her.

Take today, for instance. A surge of desire had rushed through him the moment she had entered the conference room. And when their gazes had connected it seemed that every nerve ending in his body had awakened.

Drawing in a deep breath, he forced one foot in front of the other as he made his way into the kitchen. Tonight would be one of those nights when dinner would be a guessing game and frankly he wasn't in the mood. He could have stopped somewhere to eat before coming home, but this was one night he wanted to put as much distance between him and the hospital as he could.

The day hadn't gotten off to a good start. The moment he'd entered the hospital and been told Dr. Dudley needed to see him immediately, he'd gotten a clue how things would be. Because Lucien had been the one to actually terminate Terrence, his name would come under fire as well. The thought of the Matthewses actually filing a suit against the hospital when they knew their son had a drug problem was ludicrous. It only went to show that people with money thought they could do just about anything.

Lucien opened his freezer and pulled out a microwave dinner. Moments later while waiting for his meal to heat up he decided to switch his thoughts to more pleasant things.

Namely, Jaclyn Campbell.

After the morning meeting with Dr. Dudley, they had met again when one of her patients, Marvin Spencer, had presented with shortness of breath and she needed approval to increase the dosage of the man's medication. As usual she was precise and right on point. There was no doubt in his mind that she would become an outstanding physician. On her previous rotations she'd received nothing but compliments from patients and fellow doctors alike. Patients felt she listened to what they'd had to say, and doctors remarked on her professionalism.

His thoughts shifted back to their time in Mr. Spencer's room. They had worked well together, adjusting the intravenous line, asking the patient questions.

Jerome Stubbs, a male nurse who usually worked in O.R., had also been in the room. But even while Lucien was checking Mr. Spencer's vital signs, the only person he had been aware of was Jaclyn. The first time it happened had been her first day at Hopewell, over a year ago. He'd gotten upset with himself for his immediate attraction to her, and he still wasn't sure what had brought it on. For some reason the sight of her in her pale blue scrubs had been a total turn-on.

Later that week, when the staff had joined the interns offsite at a nearby bar and grill for a casual get-acquainted session, all it had taken was seeing the way her body had been shaped by a pair of denim jeans and a pullover sweater, and his mouth had watered for days.

And then he had run into her at a grocery store one Sunday. She had been dressed for church and he'd gotten a chance to see the most gorgeous pair of legs any woman could own. She had looked so good in her peach-colored fashionable two-piece suit that he had only narrowly avoided running his grocery cart into a display of canned goods in the middle of the aisle.

Never had any woman been able to dominate his attention like she had, especially in the workplace. And no matter how much he'd tried, he hadn't been able to lick his inappropriate attention for the female doctor who was reporting to him directly. And that wasn't good.

The bummer was that the attraction was one-sided. There was not one incident he could cite as being deliberate on her part. She had the type of beauty a woman didn't have to flaunt. It was just there and he honestly doubted she knew the effect she had on men.

Hell, he'd even seen Dr. Dudley eye her down more than once and had to bite down the jealousy that had consumed him. But then the old man was known to have that bad-ass habit with the female interns. Lucien was surprised no one had filed a sexual harassment complaint against him. Lucien wasn't blind. He'd seen the looks and heard Dudley's offhand comments to several of the female interns. He'd even confronted his superior about his behavior, which hadn't gone over well.

As he sat down to dine alone, his thoughts shifted back to Jaclyn Campbell. He'd assumed he had fixed his problem when he'd sent her to work the nightshift in E.R. for a while. Usually she would have left the hospital by the time he would arrive. But on one particular morning there had been a school bus accident resulting in a number of injured kids. E.R. had been quite busy that day and everyone, even off-duty personnel, had been called in to assist.

And he had seen her. He had worked alongside her that day, and finally admitted to himself that he didn't want distance between them again. He would just have to learn how to control his attraction. So far he had. However, there were days, like today, that could test him to the fullest.

While they were in Mr. Spencer's room together, he had looked at her face and thought she was the most beautiful woman in the world. He'd seen the long dark lashes and how they'd fanned across her face, her beautiful hazel eyes, her chin-length, straight brown hair and creamy fair skin. Although she'd never confirmed or denied it, he'd heard that she was the product of a biracial marriage. Her father's family hailed from Scotland and her mother was African-American.

After completing his meal, he stood to stretch his body when his cell phone rang. He smiled when he pulled the iPhone from his back pocket and saw the caller was his sister.

"Yeah, kiddo?"

"Everyone, especially Nana, will be particularly glad to hear you're coming home for Christmas. Tell me it's true, Lucien."

He chuckled. Although both he and his sister were naturalized citizens of the United States, "home" was their birthplace of Jamaica. He, his sister, Lori, and a slew of cousins had all left Jamaica about the same time to attend college in the United States and had eventually made it their home. But for the holidays everyone tried returning for what they considered a family reunion. Due to work obligations he'd missed attending the last two years.

"It's only August, Lori. Any reason you want to know so soon? You've got four months."

"Four months will be here before you know it, Lu. Besides, we need time to plan and to prepare Nana for the disappointment if you aren't coming again. It will be three years. I wish you can make it this year."

Lucien didn't have to be reminded. His grandmother did that every time they spoke. He hadn't been home since he'd taken the position of chief resident at the hospital. With the job came new obligations as well as a number of sacrifices.

He smiled. "You'll get your wish, Lori. I'm going home for the holidays. The time off is already on the hospital schedule."

Not wanting to risk getting a busted eardrum, he held the phone from his ear when she began screaming in excitement. He was older than his sister by a year and they had always been close, although they now lived thousands of miles apart. She was an attorney working and living in Los Angeles.

He placed the phone back to his ear when he felt it was safe to do so. "Doesn't take much to get you excited, does it?"

"Oh, you," she admonished softly. "This is great news, so don't try to downplay it. Nana is going to be counting the days."

And he would, too. As far as he was concerned his grandmother was the wisest women he knew and always had been. And she was the kindest and most motivating. Not only had she raised Lucien, but she had also supported everything he'd ever wanted to do and had extended this same support to his sister and his two cousins whom she'd also raised. That's why one of the first things the four of them had done after achieving their goals in America was to build Nana a beautiful and spacious home in Kingston, Jamaica, that had a picturesque view of the Blue Mountains from every room.

A short while later Lucien ended the call with Lori, looking forward to the two weeks he would be home. But he had a lot to do before he left Alexandria for Kingston. He had to get some normalcy in his life. And the way to achieve that goal was to get a handle on his attraction to Jaclyn Campbell. He'd tried it before and it hadn't worked. This time, no matter what, he couldn't fail.

Because he knew if he did, he was headed for deep trouble.

Chapter 2

"Have you given any more thought to my suggestion that we get a puppy, Jaclyn?"

Jaclyn glanced across the stretcher at her roommate Isabelle Morales as they quickly rolled a pregnant woman down the hall toward the delivery room. A Jennifer Lopez look-alike, Isabelle wanted to go into pediatrics when her residency ended, and Jaclyn considered her friend one of the brightest interns at Hopewell.

"I honestly don't think a puppy is a good idea, Isabelle. With the hours we spend at the hospital who's going to make sure he's fed properly?" she replied.

Before Isabelle could respond, the patient, who'd been enduring her labor pains quietly, suddenly screamed. She had been in labor for the past ten hours and, last timed, her contractions were less than three minutes apart. Her obstetrician was already in the delivery room waiting.

"The two of you are talking about puppies and I'm about to die here," the woman snarled at them.

"You're not dying, Mrs. White, you're having a baby."

Ignoring what Jaclyn said, the woman then added, "And where is my husband?"

"He's washing up. He'll be in the delivery room when we get there," Isabelle added.

"I don't want him there. He's the one responsible for my condition."

Jaclyn cast a glance over at Isabelle and fought back a smile. She pitied Mr. White about now.

As soon as they wheeled the mother-to-be through the double doors, several nurses took over. One of them was Jerome. "It took both of you to bring her here?" he asked grinning. "Better not let Miss Thang see you. She'll think you're goofing off with nothing better to do."

"I was on break," Isabelle said smiling. "Besides, I needed to talk to Jaclyn about something."

At that moment Dr. De Winter walked out of the operating room and Jaclyn had to quickly compose herself. The man did things to her without even trying. Not that he would try because he didn't have the same interest in her that she had in him.

He stopped before them. "Dr. Morales and Dr. Campbell. How are you two doing?"

"Fine," they responded simultaneously.

He looked solely at Isabelle. "Dr. Morales, Dr. Thornton

has requested that one of my interns be ready to assist him tomorrow. He's performing an advanced surgical procedure on the throat of a six-year-old boy. Is that something you'd be interested in?"

Jaclyn thought the smile on Isabelle's face was priceless. "Yes, sir. Very much so," she said in an excited voice.

"Then be here ready to scrub up at eight in the morning."

"Thanks. I will."

"Good." And without saying anything else, or giving Jaclyn a second glance, he walked off.

Jaclyn's gaze followed him until he was no longer in sight. She then switched her attention back to Isabelle who was grinning from ear to ear. Dr. De Winter's recommendation that one of his interns be present during surgery was a big thing and every intern under him knew it.

"That's a good opportunity, Isabelle. Congratulations."

"Thanks. I can't believe he chose me."

Jaclyn chuckled. "I can. He recognizes how good you are and knows you're planning to go into pediatrics. You deserve it."

The smile slowly faded from Isabelle's face. "Not everyone will think so."

Jaclyn knew that to be true. Not all the interns were supportive of each other. Some were competitive and a few were downright cutthroat.

"Hey, don't worry about it. A few might bitch and

moan, but I doubt any of them will question Dr. De Winter about it," Jaclyn said.

"You're right, but—"

"No buts, Isabelle."

Later, when Jaclyn made her rounds, she turned the corner and collided head-on with Dr. De Winter, sending the charts she was carrying flying across the floor. "Oh, I'm sorry. I wasn't looking where I was going."

"Apparently, Dr. Campbell," he said in what she thought was an ultra-sexy voice. It was the same voice that she'd heard in her dreams last night, the night before and the night before that.

He knelt down and began picking up her charts and she knelt to join him. "You don't have to do that, Dr. De Winter. I can get them."

"No problem," he said, handing her the charts he'd collected.

Their gazes connected the moment their fingers touched and she felt a deep stirring in the pit of her stomach. As she stared into his eyes she thought she saw them darken, but when she blinked he'd already straightened and was standing back up.

She stood as well. "Thank you," she murmured, clutching the charts to her chest like an armor of steel.

"You're welcome. And how are your patients? Any problems or concerns?"

Because he'd asked... "There is this one thing. We're still trying to determine the reason behind Mr. Aiken's high fevers."

Dr. De Winter nodded. "I understand he had another one this morning."

"Yes. We took more blood, but there's nothing abnormal. The fever means there's infection somewhere in his body, but nothing is showing up in his blood."

"So you're dealing with an FUO?"

Fever of unknown origin. "Yes," she said, clearly disturbed.

"Any other signs and symptoms, Dr. Campbell?"

"None."

"Let me see his chart for a second."

She pushed a lock of hair behind her ear and then flipped through the charts to find the one belonging to William Aiken. She handed it to Dr. De Winter, grateful their fingers did not touch this time.

Her pulse thudded as she stood there and watched him peruse the man's chart. She couldn't help noticing how his long lashes fanned across his cheeks and how sensuous his mouth looked. He then glanced up and caught her staring at his mouth. *Good grief.*

"May I make a suggestion, Dr. Campbell?"

"Yes, sir, you may." The one thing that was different about Dr. De Winter compared to other doctors in an authoritative position was that he didn't project a brash, all-knowing demeanor. He liked getting input from the interns he supervised and always solicited their opinions.

"Have blood drawn from his toe, preferably the big one, and have it checked."

She raised a brow. Probably any other intern would have accepted what he said without question, but unfortunately she wasn't one of them. "Why, if I may ask?"

He chuckled and the sound seemed to whisper across

her skin. "Yes, doctor, you may. When I was an intern at a college in Boston, I had a patient with FUO and drawing blood from the big toe was suggested to me by the chief of staff. He explained that often bad blood will find places to settle and can't easily be detected."

She nodded as understanding dawned. "Which was the premise behind bloodletting," she said, thinking out loud and seeing his point. "Which is the draining of bad blood out of a person's body. And if there's bad blood not detected, it might be confined in one of the body's peripheral points. A premise we have now put to sound scientific use."

"Exactly."

She smiled. "Thanks, Dr. De Winter. I'll have that done immediately." She then quickly walked away.

Lucien watched Jaclyn hurry off and drew in a deep breath. When they had accidentally touched moments ago, it had taken everything within him to control the urge to pull her into his arms and mesh his lips with hers. That encounter had been too close for comfort. Way too close.

No matter how much he tried to control himself around her, he was finding it hard to do so. When they had knelt facing each other and he'd looked into her eyes and gazed upon the lushness of her mouth, heat had flared inside of him. He could imagine them kneeling facing each other, but the setting hadn't been the hall of the hospital. In his mind they were in the middle of the bed. Naked.

Those were the last kind of thoughts he needed

lodged in his brain. He tried forcing them out. The hospital's nonfraternization policy had been put in place for a reason and he intended to abide by it. But God, he was attracted to her. And if knowing that wasn't enough to shake his world, then he didn't know what would. At that moment he thought he could even feel the floor shift under his feet. Yes, he was definitely standing on shaky ground.

Jaclyn nibbled on her bottom lip as she read Mr. Aiken's most recent lab report. Dr. De Winter had been right in suggesting that blood be drawn from the man's toe. The report clearly indicated bacteria in Mr. Aiken's body. Bacteria of an unknown source.

Now she had to determine what was causing it. As she read the report again the main question circling around in her head was why the bacteria hadn't shown up in a routine lab test.

"You're too pretty to be frowning."

Jaclyn glanced up and smiled at Ravi Patel, another intern. With his tall, slender build, long wavy black hair, dark eyes and dark skin, he made a reality of the old cliché tall, dark and handsome.

All the female interns, nurses and patients alike drooled over the American-born East Indian. Even Miss Thang seemed taken with him and would blush like a silly schoolgirl whenever Ravi was near. What Jaclyn most admired and respected about Ravi was that he was quick to let the admiring ladies know that he was an engaged man. His fiancée, a woman from India, was an intern at a hospital in Miami. The two planned to marry in a few years.

"Hi, Ravi. I was going over one of my patient's charts."

"His condition is serious?"

"FUO earlier, but thanks to Dr. De Winter I was finally able to find something in his blood. There are bacteria. Now I'm trying to determine the cause."

"If you need help, this might be something to bring before the others in our group session with Dr. De Winter in the morning."

Jaclyn nibbled on her bottom lip. She of all people knew when the group of interns would meet with Dr. De Winter in a classroom setting. She looked forward to those once-a-week sessions when he would take center stage at the front of the class. Those were the times when she could sit in the back and ogle him to her heart's delight and come across only as a very attentive student.

More than once he had glanced her way and caught her staring and she appreciated that he wasn't a mind reader. He would have been appalled at some of the things she'd been thinking at the time. "I might do that. Thanks for suggesting it, Ravi."

Ravi glanced over her shoulder and smiled. "There's Dr. De Winter. We can ask him now."

Before Jaclyn could stop him, Ravi had gotten Dr. De Winter's attention. Jaclyn released a deep breath. She hadn't quite recovered from their earlier meeting when they had touched. Now he was about to get all into her space again.

"Doctors Patel and Campbell. Is there something I can help you with?" he asked, his gaze passing between them.

"Yes, sir," Jaclyn said. "Thanks to your suggestion I was able to pinpoint bacteria in Mr. Aiken's blood. But now I'm concerned with the cause. I've done tests to rule out several abnormalities, but these bacteria are determined to remain in certain areas. I'm still concerned that we could not detect it in a routine blood test."

"I thought this would be something she could bring before the group in the morning," Ravi interjected.

"I agree with Dr. Patel. This is something we can give the group as a think tank question, Dr. Campbell. In the meantime, how is Mr. Aiken? What are we doing for him?"

Before Jaclyn could respond, Ravi glanced at his watch and then said apologetically, "Sorry, I need to go check on one of my patients."

He then quickly walked off leaving her alone with Dr. De Winter. She forced her gaze from Ravi's retreating back to Dr. De Winter. For the next few minutes she provided him with the answer to his question. He didn't interrupt and every so often he would nod slowly. It was hard not to get absorbed in the tingles of awareness that were going through her body from his standing so close to her.

At one point while she was talking, their eyes held for a moment. Her mind went completely blank and it was only when he'd said in a warm tone, "You were saying, Dr. Campbell?" that she realized she had stopped talking in mid-sentence. She swallowed hard and began talking again, knowing with her fair skin that her blush of embarrassment was easy to see.

So okay, now he knew one of his interns was taken with him. The man was sexy and handsome so there was no doubt in her mind she wasn't the first and wouldn't be the last. Although flattered, he was a professional who wouldn't encourage her. He probably considered her one of those silly little interns with hormonal problems. For her it went beyond that. Oh, she would love to jump his bones if given the chance, but her crush on him was growing by leaps and bounds each day.

When she finally finished her spiel, he met her gaze and asked in what she thought was a husky voice, "Why did you zone out on me a few moments ago?"

She hadn't expected him to ask her that. Did he honestly expect her to tell him the truth? Even worse, did he suspect the truth? She drew in a deep breath and decided to lie through her teeth. "No reason, sir. I merely lost my train of thought for a second." *And please don't ask me why.*

He slowly nodded and as if he could read her mind and was privy to her last thought, he took a step back. "I'll see you at the group discussion in the morning, Dr. Campbell."

And then he walked away.

Chapter 3

Jaclyn had known the moment she entered the meeting room the next morning and saw how everyone was clustered together and talking in whispers that word was out about the Matthews lawsuit.

It had been bad enough when everyone had found out about Terrence's termination last month. Speculation had run wild as to the reason for it. Now his family was bringing things out in the open and letting everyone know what was going on and that the hospital would pay for what they saw as a grave mistake.

"Hey, what's going on?" she asked a fellow intern by the name of Tamara St. John as she slid into the seat beside her. She'd liked Tamara from the first day they met and found her to be a down-to-earth person.

Tamara leaned closer and whispered, "Word is out as to the real reason Terrence was kicked out of the program. Rumor has it that he had a drug problem. His family is suing the hospital and saying the charges against him are false."

Jaclyn swallowed deeply. "What will the hospital do?"

"I hear they feel they have a good case against Terrence. Someone on staff came forward with the goods on him and provided enough proof to make the hospital take action. Now everyone is trying to figure out who among us talked."

A muscle tightened in Jaclyn's stomach. "Does it matter, especially if the allegations are true?" she asked.

"Doesn't matter to me. I can't help admiring the person for doing it. Some people who are born into wealth think they can get away with anything. Terrence acted like too much of a snob to suit me anyway."

Tamara glanced beyond Jaclyn and smiled. "Here comes Dr. De Winter. We'll talk later." Tamara then straightened in her seat to chime in with the others when they said, "Good morning, Dr. De Winter."

"Good morning, everyone," the husky voice replied.

Jaclyn hadn't been one of those to coo out the greeting, yet she thought his gaze deliberately settled on her as he passed her seat to walk toward the front of the room. It was then that she overheard a female intern sitting in front of her whisper to another woman, "That doctor is way too fine. I just love watching him strut his stuff."

Jaclyn thought the same thing. She liked seeing him strut his stuff as well, but that was something she wouldn't dare share with anyone. She watched and listened as he went through the regular routine of asking how things were going and if anyone had had any challenges for the week to share with the others.

She knew that was her cue and she raised her hand. He glanced over in her direction. "Yes, Dr. Campbell?"

She spoke up and presented Mr. Aiken's situation to everyone. Some fellow interns asked questions while jotting down notes. Several threw out possible diagnoses for her to consider and she wrote those down as well. It was nice getting feedback from her peers. More than once she glanced at Dr. De Winter and saw him watching and listening with interest. He was letting them work as a team. A few times it seemed after scanning the room his gaze would come to settle on her. And each time it did, her breath would get caught in her throat and she would swallow deeply to force the air down.

"So, Dr. Campbell, do you think you have enough possibilities to work with?" he asked, his eyes homing in on hers in a way that made blood rush through her veins.

She took a deep breath and then responded, "Yes, and I'm going to narrow it down to the best three."

He nodded. "Time might not be on your side," Dr. De Winter then said. "I understand Mr. Aiken's fever spiked overnight."

She wasn't surprised that he was well aware of what was going on with each of the intern's patients under his charge. How he kept up with it all she didn't know. There were fifteen of them and each had been assigned five to seven patients.

"Yes, sir, but so far we're keeping the temperature down."

He nodded. "But what we want is to get rid of it all together."

Jaclyn moistened her lips with her tongue thinking she could have taken his words as a put-down. Instead she took them as a challenge. A patient's health was on the line and her job as a doctor was to not make him comfortable but to get him well. "Yes, sir."

He straightened from the podium he'd been leaning against and then looked out over the group. "Good job, team. Now go out there and take care of your patients."

Lucien remained behind in the empty meeting room. Things with Jaclyn Campbell were still not going well. Hooking up with a woman, getting to know her, developing a relationship both mentally and especially physically, was one of those simple pleasures in life that all men looked forward to experiencing.

He dated, although it had been a while since he'd dated anyone seriously. He always enjoyed a female's company, but in most situations he tried avoiding dating women in his own profession. More often than not their conversations would center too much around the medical cases they were up against.

The last woman he'd dated had been in the education field and he enjoyed learning about her work and the challenges she faced. The only bad thing about Shawnee Powers was her inability to stop placing herself on some sort of pedestal. There was nothing wrong with someone believing in themselves, but for Shawnee it had begun getting downright ridiculous. He'd put up with it until he'd noticed her jealous streak. She had begun questioning him when he didn't call or when he didn't immediately text her back. It had been ten months since they'd broken up and at no time had he been tempted to call her.

Ten months.

That had been when he'd seen Jaclyn for the first time. He would always remember that day. There had been twenty residents and now they were down to fifteen. One had gotten seriously sick and had to leave the program, three hadn't been able to cope the first six months and one he'd had to terminate.

His mind shifted to Terrence Matthews, the one he'd had to terminate. The young man, although somewhat brash at times, had had a promising future. He had started off sharp as a whip, up on every assignment and possessed a bedside manner all the patients appreciated. Then Terrence began being late to group meetings, going MIA when he was supposed to be visiting patients and falling asleep during group discussions.

Lucien had mentioned Terrence's behavior to Dr. Dudley who at first hadn't wanted to rock the boat; after all the man was a Matthews. But Lucien had been making his own notes and observations when Jaclyn had come to him about Terrence's drug use.

Without Terrence aware he was being observed, she had witnessed him stealing drugs from the hospital pharmacy. A replay of the pharmacy's surveillance camera had backed up her claim, and a random drug test confirmed Terrence's drug use.

Lucien shook his head when he recalled the day he had summoned Dr. Matthews to his office. The man didn't deny the charges. Instead he said because he was a Matthews and his family had given so much to the hospital, he felt anything he did should and could be overlooked.

Even the offer that he take a temporary leave and go into drug rehab was laughed off with Terrence saying to do such a thing would be an admission of guilt. Lucien had ending up terminating Terrence's association with the hospital that day.

Although he'd backed up Lucien's actions, Dr. Dudley had predicted there would be a backlash from the Matthews family. The old man had been right.

Drawing in a deep breath Lucien walked to the window and glanced out at downtown Alexandria. Below, the brick-paved streets were lined with shops and boutiques of early eighteenth and nineteenth century architecture. And in the distance, across the Potomac, was the nation's capital in all its glorious splendor. He enjoyed where he worked and loved living in Georgetown, far enough from the hospital on the D.C. side to appreciate the days he had off work.

He knew Jaclyn lived in Virginia, and the only times their paths had crossed after hours had been that Sunday when he'd decided to do his grocery shopping at a store in Alexandria.

He rubbed his hand down his face and turned away from the window. Although she had been sitting in the back of the room today, his gaze had sought her out anyway. He had looked for her. Found her. And had felt his attraction to her intensify. When she'd opened her mouth to speak, his pulse had accelerated and his ability to breathe had become affected.

What the hell was wrong with him?

It had taken all of his control to keep his features neutral, void of expression. Each and every time he was around her he risked the possibility of giving something away. The interns under his charge were bright, observant and astute. They would hang on to his every word, decipher his every action.

Jaclyn made it hard for him to think straight at times. Like today when she had been explaining Mr. Aiken's condition to everyone. While she talked about the man's fever, Lucien had begun imagining a fever of a different kind—the typed generated in the heat of passion between a man and a woman. Namely, him and her. He could envision her lush body, naked and hot, extremely hot, writhing beneath his while he thrust in and out of her making nonstop love to her.

Those thoughts had been the last thing that should have been flowing through his mind, but they weren't. Even now those kinds of thoughts were uppermost in his mind and determined to get the best of him. It might be wise to consider placing as much distance between him and Jaclyn as possible, and the only way he could do that was to suggest she transfer to another hospital. He knew there was no way he could do that. It wouldn't be fair to her to disrupt her position here just because he was the one with a libido problem.

As he gathered his belongings, Lucien knew what

he had to do. He had to get a grip. No matter what, he could not lower his guard around her.

By lunchtime Jaclyn had heard so many versions of what was going down with the Matthews lawsuit that she wondered where was rumor control when you needed it. The only good thing was that so far no one knew the identity of the person who'd snitched on Terrence and for that she was grateful.

She hadn't known what to expect when she'd made the decision to come forward to report Terrence's drug abuse. But her parents had raised her to do the right thing, and knowing about the abuse and the harm it could cause her fellow doctor had been the determining factor in making her talk. No one knew she was the one responsible for Terrence losing his job. Not even her roommate Isabelle.

No one except Dr. De Winter.

Just the mention of his name made a picture of him flash in her mind. He was so drop-dead gorgeous. Most of the other female staffers felt the same way, too. She'd heard the comments, and she'd noticed that several of them would cook up any excuse to go up to his office, only to return with what they considered the same disappointing news. Dr. De Winter had suspected them from the first. In other words, he'd seen through their attempt at shrewdness and wasn't having any of it.

Thoughts of Dr. De Winter still took up residence in her mind hours later at the end of her shift. But they'd been pushed to the background after she'd overheard some interns trying to figure out who had nailed Terrence. They had what they termed a snitch among them.

They'd claimed if they'd known about Terrence, they would have implemented a "don't ask, don't tell" policy. Who in their right mind would want to go up against the Matthews family? they'd asked. Hadn't the snitch caused the hospital more harm than good now that the family was withdrawing its financial support?

As far as Jaclyn was concerned things were getting out of hand. What if Dr. Dudley was wrong and she was identified as the person who'd come forward about Terrence? She could see some of the interns turning on her and making her life at Hopewell unpleasant.

She knew the one person she needed to talk with and found him standing at a nurse's station writing in a patient's chart. Taking a deep breath she walked over to him. "Excuse me, Dr. De Winter, may I speak with you privately?"

Lucien stopped writing at the sound of the soft feminine voice. He didn't have to glance up to see to whom it belonged. He forced the air from his lungs as he turned and looked into Jaclyn's face. He immediately saw from the look in her eyes that she was troubled by something. But he had to play it cool, remembering he couldn't jump at the chance to be alone with her any more than he would any of the other interns.

He stuck his pen into his pocket and lifted a brow. "I'm about to call it a day, Dr. Campbell. Is it something that can wait until tomorrow?" he asked in a no-nonsense, very professional tone, knowing his words had been overheard by Nurse Tsang who was all ears.

As usual her radar was on high alert. The woman had a tendency to mind everyone's business but her own.

"No, sir. It can't wait."

He glanced at his watch. "Very well, then. We can go to my office."

They walked side by side toward his office at the end of the corridor. And with every step he took he inhaled her scent. The tropical fragrance of jasmine reminded him of the night-blooming flower from the island where he'd been born. She was wearing it well and it made him recall sultry summer nights.

As he walked beside her, he racked his brain for something to say that wouldn't come out as too forward. He glanced over at her. With her exotic features and dark hair, she could pass for an island girl if it wasn't for her fair skin. She was a beauty. He'd thought so the first time he'd seen her and he thought so now.

He increased his pace and she managed to keep up with him. Lucien could imagine those long legs beneath the slacks could do so with ease.

It had been a quiet day, no emergencies that had needed his attention beyond the norm and for that he was grateful. He had been about to call it a day, had hoped he could quietly slip out without seeing her more than he already had that day. But now it seemed he would be in close quarters with her. As long as he kept things on a professional note he would be fine.

At least that was his prayer.

But his prayer didn't help him a few minutes later when they'd reached his office and he held the door open for her to enter. She brushed past him and her scent had made him tremble.

He knew at that moment he had no business bringing her to his office. The space was tight as it was and having her in it would make it even more confining. And as he stepped into the cramped room behind her and closed the door, he knew he was in trouble.

Deep trouble.

Jaclyn glanced around the office, remembering the first time she had been here. That had been her first week at the hospital and Nurse Tsang had reported to Dr. De Winter that she hadn't turned in her end-of-the-day report on time. Jaclyn had argued that her report had been turned in on time, but Nurse Tsang's watch had been set two minutes early. Dr. De Winter had calmly suggested that to eliminate confusion in the future she get her report in five minutes early. What he hadn't said and what she clearly understood that day was that the head nurse enjoyed making everyone's lives miserable and she'd have to avoid getting caught in her trap.

Jaclyn took a deep breath when she remembered the last time she'd been in his office. It was last month when she had reported Terrence's drug use. She had done a lot of soul searching before requesting a meeting with Dr. De Winter and now it looked like the decision she'd made that day might be coming back to haunt her.

"Please have a seat, Dr. Campbell."

"Thank you." She sat in the chair next to his desk and she watched as he sat down as well.

"If you're here regarding the remark I made earlier today in the group session, it wasn't made to call you out or to make it seem as if you didn't know what needed to be done."

She shook her head. "Yes, I know, but that's not why I'm here," she said softly.

He nodded. "Then why are you here? You said whatever you needed to talk to me about couldn't wait until tomorrow."

She inhaled deeply again, wondering why the man had to look so heartthrob sexy. She'd been around good-looking men before, but there was something about Dr. De Winter's looks that could literally take a woman's breath away. She wondered if he knew the effect he had on women and decided yes, he had to know.

"Dr. Campbell?"

She blinked, realizing he was waiting for her to say something. "They are talking."

He raised his brow and a guarded look appeared on his face, and she wondered the reason. "Who's talking?"

"Everyone. They know. Or they think they know and those who don't are trying to figure it out."

He leaned back in his chair and simply stared at her, but it was a stare that made tiny flutters appear in her stomach. "I think you need to tell me just what you're talking about," he said in a gentle tone, so gentle it made her want to tell him everything, especially her misgivings about letting him know about Terrence and how everyone was trying to figure out just who told. But she wanted to go even farther and spill her guts about how she felt about him, how she dreamed about him at night and how she often envisioned him naked. Most important, how her desire and love for him kept taunting her day in and day out. However, she knew she couldn't tell him any of those things. She wouldn't dare.

"I'm talking about the Matthews lawsuit," she finally said. "That's all everyone has been talking about all morning. They're determined to find out who snitched on Terrence."

"They won't."

"Can you be absolutely sure of that, Dr. De Winter?" she asked in frustration, fighting back tears that threatened to fall any minute. When she'd come to him to report Terrence's problem she had hoped that in addition to protecting the hospital in the long run she would be protecting Terrence as well. He needed help. She knew firsthand what drugs could do to a person and didn't want an addiction to rule his life like it had ruled her brother's, Kevin's.

"Yes, I can be absolutely sure of it, Dr. Campbell. You are protected by the privacy act. What you told me was in confidence and that is equivalent to doctor-patient privilege. I don't have to reveal my source to anyone. Besides, it doesn't matter. He didn't pass the random drug test that was given to him that day."

"I know, but what if their attorneys force the issue? Then what? I thought I was doing the right thing in telling you about it, but now I—"

"You were doing the right thing. You knew one of your fellow interns was involved in something unethical and you brought it to my attention. I repeat, you did the right thing."

There was something in his gentle and understanding tone that pushed her to the edge. There were so many emotions she was trying to deal with. The issue with Terrence was just one of her problems. But beside all that, her feelings for the gorgeous doctor was another issue all together. She'd always been pretty level-headed when it came to men, but she felt way out of her league with Lucien De Winter, mainly because she knew she'd fallen in love with him the moment she'd set eyes on him. She was too old to consider it merely a schoolgirl crush. She'd stop thinking of it in those terms months ago. She was experiencing the wants, desires and needs of a woman with the man she loved.

Now there was no telling what would happen. Once word got out she was the snitch, the hospital would probably have to send her away to downplay all the negative publicity. That meant she wouldn't see Lucien ever again. She would leave without his having a clue how she felt about him. But what did it matter? she asked herself. Her feelings weren't reciprocated.

"Look, maybe I should not have requested this meeting today," she said standing, unable to fight the tears any longer. The do-gooder didn't always save the day, she reminded herself. Not all the time. "I have to go," she said swiping at the tears falling from her eyes.

He stood as well. "No, not this way. Not with tears. I don't want to see you cry."

In a move that surprised her, he stepped around his desk and pulled her into his arms. The moment he wrapped his arms around her, giving her a shoulder to cry on, she took it and began sobbing.

"Shh, things are going to be all right. You're going to have to trust me. The Matthewses will eventually discover that money can't buy everything."

Jaclyn knew for her to be standing here sobbing her heart out in her supervisor's arms was inappropriate, but she couldn't pull away. He smelled good and the way his hand was gently stroking her back felt wonderful.

And then, as if he realized where they were and what he was doing, his hand stilled. She swallowed and lifted her head from his chest to take a step back. But instead of letting her go, he reached out and tenderly cupped her chin in his hand and forced their gazes to connect.

The look she saw in his eyes had her senses reeling. At the same time sexual tension, as thick as it could get, began surrounding them, capturing them in a mist that was saturated with desire. She felt it and knew he had to feel it as well. If it wasn't for the beat of her heart marking the passage of time she would not have known how long they'd been standing there, staring at each other with deep hunger entrenched in their gazes and heat radiating between them.

He moved closer and slowly began lowering his head until his warm breath fanned across her lips. She wanted to blink but couldn't. His hot, possessive gaze was keeping her eyes wide open and glued to his. Her pulse quickened with every inch closer to her mouth that his lips came.

The room was charged with something she'd never experienced before, a kind of static electricity that increased the flow of blood rushing through her veins, made her world turn upside-down, then right-side up. His hand on her chin began moving, allowing his knuckles to tenderly caress the side of her jaw. Her vision blurred when a heated sensation took over her senses and every part of her body.

He lowered his head still more and his mouth came within a breath of taking possession of her lips. Suddenly the alarm on his desk sounded and they knew what that meant: 911 in E.R.

Without saying anything they both rushed toward the door.

Chapter 4

Lucien glanced around. E.R. was in chaos. Doors were flying open with people being wheeled in on stretchers. He stopped one of the nurses. "What do we have?"

"Twelve-car pileup on the interstate. There were four casualties on impact—three of them children in different families. Life flight is on its way and rescue is unloading others as we speak," she said.

"We need all hands on board. Contact all medical staff, even those off duty," Lucien said. He then raced off to assist an injured teenager. Jaclyn was right on his heels. Lucien treated one patient after another, seeing to everyone's needs, and making sure those needing surgery were taken care of.

He glanced over at Jaclyn and saw she was busy as well and couldn't help admire how she was handling things. He had a feeling this would be a long day.

* * *

It was close to four in the morning before things had settled down in the E.R. Jaclyn thought it was so quiet the place appeared eerie. Of the thirty-four people who'd been involved in the twelve-car accident, six hadn't survived and four were still in critical condition. The others had been fortunate to receive minor injuries.

She couldn't help but be proud of her fellow doctors and how they had handled each patient swiftly, confidently, compassionately. Then there had been the media who had swarmed inside looking for a story. And then the family members who'd come to see for themselves that their loved ones were all right. Through it all, she admired the way Dr. De Winter had handled himself and the entire situation. Now she knew why he was one of the top physicians at the hospital and especially why he was in charge of the interns. They respected him and when it counted they had pulled together to make it happen and had saved lives.

She felt good. Exhausted but good. This was the career she had chosen and helping others gave her a high.

A shiver ran through her when she recalled what had almost taken place in his office, right before the alarm had sounded. She refused to believe she had imagined the heat and the desire she had seen in his eyes. It had been real. And he had come within seconds of kissing her.

She pulled her tired body out of the chair beside a patient's stretcher. Ten-month-old Stacia Minestrone, the youngest survivor of the multicar accident, had only minor injuries but was waiting for a bed in Pediatrics. Even though she was presently under Tamara's care, Jaclyn had agreed to observe the precious little girl while Tamara touched base with family services. Stacia's mother hadn't survived and the little girl's father who lived in Wisconsin had been notified and was on his way.

Jaclyn glanced up when Tamara returned. "Thanks for watching her for me. I guess you're ready to leave this place about now."

Jaclyn stood, stretched her muscles and glanced at her watch. She was to have gotten off work more than eight hours ago. Tamara had been spared the initial arrival of E.R. patients because she'd been assisting in O.R. But like the others, once she'd arrived she had quickly joined in to do what was needed to be done.

"Yes, I can't wait to get home to my bed," Jaclyn said. "I'm going to the locker for my backpack and then I'm out of here."

It didn't take her long to gather her things. She was on her way out the hospital's revolving doors when Dr. De Winter called out, "Dr. Campbell, wait up."

She turned around and the moment she did so, her pulse quickened at the sight of him jogging toward her. He had removed his lab coat and was wearing jeans and a shirt. She wondered if he was aware of the effect he had on women, especially the effect he had on her.

The man exuded so much raw masculinity that she simply stood there while memories came flooding down on her. She couldn't help but recall that moment in his office when they'd almost kissed. Now that the crisis in the E.R. was over, she fully understood her predicament. No matter what almost happened in his office, which she still hadn't gotten over, she was an intern and Dr. De Winter was her boss. She would do well to remember that and not do anything to put her job and her career in jeopardy. That was probably why he was in such a hurry to talk to her.

She knew what he was probably going to say. She'd been crying and he'd only taken her into his arms as a way to comfort her and nothing else. Anything else that she assumed she saw or thought transpired was a figment of her imagination.

When he came to a stop in front of her a lock of hair fell in her face and she pushed it away at the same moment she shifted her backpack to another shoulder. "Yes, Dr. De Winter. Is there something you need me to do before I leave?"

Lucien thought that was a loaded question if ever there was one. He could easily respond by saying yes, there was something he needed her to do before she left. Returning to his office so they could finish what they'd started earlier would be nice.

Then he could take her mouth, make love to it, mate with it without any distractions or interruptions. Or if she didn't want to go to his office, they could go anywhere. She could name the place and he wouldn't hesitate to take her there.

"No, there isn't anything I need for you to do," he said, studying her features. She looked tired, but exhaustion in no way detracted from her beauty. "You did a hell of a job in there today. I appreciate everything you and the other interns did. The group was awesome."

One thing Lucien subscribed to was that it didn't pay to bully his group of interns. He was not one who believed in group spankings. He dealt with those individually who did not pull their weight. On the others he didn't mind bestowing compliments when they were due. After what had gone down in E.R., praise was certainly called for. He would tell her now and the others when he saw them again.

Although he'd given her a compliment, what was on his mind more now than anything else was the kiss they'd almost shared in his office. A part of him knew in a way he should be grateful it didn't happen and regret that it almost did. But the truth of the matter was that the memory of holding her in his arms, inhaling her scent, bringing his lips so close to hers sent a flood of heat rushing through his veins and made his breath catch in his throat.

"Thanks," she said. "You did an outstanding job yourself. It amazes me how well you do what you do and know just when to do it, seemingly without thought."

He chuckled. "It comes with practice, trust me. Don't forget I was an intern once and made my share of mistakes. Thankfully none of them cost anyone their life, but still. One day you'll look back at these years and smile and accept them as your growing period."

She smiled. "I hope you're right."

"I am." He glanced at his watch. "I can't believe how late it is—or how early, depending on how you look at it. We never did finish our discussion from earlier today.

I know a coffee shop across the bridge that stays open twenty-four hours. This time of morning there won't be a lot of people around so we'll be able to hold a private conversation."

He paused when she hesitated in accepting his invitation. He didn't want to make her feel uncomfortable and think she had no choice in meeting with him, so he added, "Of course I'll understand if you prefer going home. You've pulled a double today so I'm sure you're tired."

Jaclyn couldn't help but smile. She doubted she could ever be tired enough to not want Lucien's company, regardless of the reason. "No, I'm fine and yes, we can finish our conversation from earlier."

In a way finishing up their conversation wasn't what she really wanted. She believed she had done the right thing in turning Terrence in, and she figured the stress, frustration and all kinds of emotions had gotten the best of her earlier and had driven her to a mental meltdown. The activities in E.R. had revived her, given her an adrenaline rush.

"You sure?" he asked.

She felt her heart slamming against her ribcage with his question. Was she absolutely, positively sure when she didn't know what he would say to her? For all she knew he might criticize her for giving in to a crying spell earlier today. But she would take her chances. "Yes, I'm sure."

He smiled. "We can take my car."

"All right."

Lucien wasn't surprised they couldn't make it out

of the hospital and to the parking lot without encountering someone he'd rather not have seen. Nurse Tsang was walking toward them as they were leaving. She stopped, causing them to do the same.

"Good morning, Ms. Tsang," he said, his tone formal.

"Dr. De Winter." The woman then glanced over at Jaclyn with a speculative eye. "Dr. Campbell."

"Good morning," Jaclyn acknowledged.

"The two of you are leaving?" the woman then asked.

Lucien lifted a brow. "Yes, we're going to get coffee. I think we've earned the right because we've been here for the last eighteen hours. We had one hell of an emergency."

"So I heard," Ms. Tsang said drily. She then looked over at Jaclyn and then back at Lucien. "Need I remind the two of you of the hospital's nonfraternization policy when it comes to managers and their subordinates?"

Lucien looked down at the woman. He smiled a little, but the smile didn't quite reach his eyes. "No. Just like I'm sure I don't have to remind you of the hospital's contact policy whenever an emergency occurs. I understand no one could reach you yesterday, Ms. Tsang. Nor did you call in."

Her gaze sharpened. "It was my long weekend and I caught the train to New York. That's why I couldn't be reached."

"I'm sure you had a nice time," he remarked.

"Yes, I did."

"Glad to hear it. Now if you will excuse us." He didn't wait to see if she would excuse them or not, nor did he care. He and Jaclyn walked off, leaving the woman standing there staring at them.

The woman had a problem with sticking her nose where it didn't belong. He had mentioned it several times to Dr. Dudley, especially when the interns had come to him complaining, but it seemed the chief of staff always found some excuse or another for Ms. Tsang.

"If you want to cancel our having coffee, I'll understand, Dr. De Winter," Jaclyn said.

He glanced over at her and he knew the smile he gave her was a lot different than the one he'd bestowed upon Ms. Tsang earlier. This one not only reached his eyes but it also spread throughout his entire body like a beacon of light. "There's no way I'm going to let Nurse Tsang's nosiness dictate what I do and how I handle my business."

He opened the car door for her, paused a moment and then asked, "I guess I'm the one who should be asking you if you still want to share a cup of coffee with me."

She smiled up at him as she slid onto the leather seat of his car. "Yes, I still want to share a cup of coffee with you."

He held her gaze. "You sure?"

She nodded. "I'm positive."

Jaclyn knew without a doubt that Lucien had no idea just how positive she was. Regardless of Nurse Tsang's remark, she had no intention of turning down Dr. De Winter's invitation to go someplace where they could talk. It didn't matter that the only discussion they would have was about the Matthews lawsuit. All she cared about was that she would be sharing his space again somewhere across the bridge that hopefully wasn't frequented by their colleagues.

"I like your car," she said after she'd buckled her seat belt and waited for him to do the same. It was a silver 1980 Trans Am, all shiny and clean and expensively upholstered.

"Thanks."

"And it sounds good. So what's under the hood?"

He glanced over at her and chuckled. "This baby was a limited edition Indy car. Turbo, 210 horsepower, 4.9 cubic inch motor and it rides like a dream."

"I hear. What's the torque?"

"Three hundred forty-five pounds."

"Um, four speed manual, V-8 and an 8-trac player that plays CDs. Very impressive, Dr. De Winter," she said.

He took his eyes off her to return to the road. "Thank you, and because we're away from the hospital a first-name basis suits me just fine." He glanced back over at her. "Is that okay with you?"

She nodded, swallowed deeply and said, "I have no problem with it."

"Okay, so tell me, Jaclyn, how do you know so much about muscle cars?"

"My dad made a living as an auto mechanic, but not just any auto mechanic. Back home people came from far and wide just to get him to look under their hoods. He was known as the Muscle Car King."

"Now I'm impressed. Where is back home?"

"Oakland, California."

"Any siblings?" he asked her.

"A brother who's four years older."

"The two of you are close?"

She chuckled. "Yes, but he stopped counting when he married a woman who became the sister I never had and they gave me a niece who everyone thinks is mine. It's uncanny, but she looks just like me when I was her age."

"Then she must be cute as a button."

"Thanks." Had he just given her a compliment? Was he insinuating he thought she was cute? She shifted positions in the seat while thinking she should probably take a chill pill because all her thoughts were wrong. *He's probably being nice to you because he doesn't want to say anything to make you burst into tears on him again.*

"Are both your parents still living?"

She chuckled. "Are they? They take the word *living* to a whole new level. At fifty my father bought a Harley and he and Mom think nothing of hitting the road crossing state lines. And then at fifty-five he bought a boat and we can't keep them off the water. He'll be sixty in a few years and my brother and I are bracing ourselves for what they'll get next."

"They sound like a fun pair."

"They are. They were high school sweethearts who married before either of them were twenty. Then they took turns going to college while raising me and my brother."

She paused a moment and then asked, "What about

you, Dr....I mean Lucien. Any siblings? Your parents still alive?"

"I have one sister. We're a year apart. And I understand both my parents are alive...somewhere."

She glanced over at him. "Don't you know?"

"No. I haven't seen my mother since I was five. She left Jamaica and swore she would never return. I was raised by my grandmother. My mother had me when she was fifteen and I never knew my father," he said quietly.

"Oh." She couldn't imagine growing up and not knowing her father because he had always been a part of her life. Although she was close to both of her parents, everyone knew she'd always been a daddy's girl.

Deciding to change the subject, she said, "I'm glad they were able to contact the father of Stacia Minestrone. I understand he and his wife divorced last year and he moved away. Her neighbor said they were trying to make a comeback and now she's gone. It's sad."

He nodded. "And what's even sadder is that according to one of the police officers involved in the investigation, the accident was caused by a twenty-year-old college student texting her boyfriend."

He paused a moment and then added, "In the end six people died, four are still critical and she was able to walk away with a few scratches. Then again maybe she won't be walking away from everything. I saw the police place her in the patrol car."

Jaclyn had seen it as well, but at the time she hadn't known why. It was sad. No, it was worse than sad. It was a sin and a shame. That text message had ended up probably being the deadliest the young woman had ever sent.

A few minutes later, Lucien pulled into a parking spot in front of a quaint-looking café of red brick with shutters at every window. Day was breaking and the sun was just coming up over the horizon. Although her budget dictated that she live outside the nation's capital, she enjoyed whenever she crossed the bridge over to D.C. And this neighborhood was the one she enjoyed the most. Georgetown, one of the oldest sections of town. She loved the tree-lined streets of old row homes drenched deep in D.C.'s history. She loved the numerous upscale boutiques, restaurants and cafés that lined the narrow cobblestoned streets. What she liked most of all was being surrounded by the beautiful flower gardens, where the cherry blossoms and gladioli were in full bloom.

Moments later they were walking through the door of a café that had only a couple of patrons sitting at the counter sipping coffee and tea. Lucien led her over to a booth in the back, and a waiter, an older man with a beard who greeted Lucien by name, quickly gave them menus.

"Nice place," Jaclyn said, deciding that in addition to a cup of coffee she'd like to try an omelet on the menu called the George Washington. It had all the ingredients she liked. Lucien told her she would not be disappointed.

Within minutes a waitress appeared to take their order. He ordered the George Washington, with coffee as well. After the waitress left, Jaclyn glanced at Lucien and smiled. "I take it you come here a lot."

He chuckled. "Practically every day. I live in the area."

"You live in Georgetown?"

"Yes. My sister lived with an older couple while attending Howard. When the couple decided to retire to Florida they gave Lori the option of buying their home before anyone else. They even financed it for her. When she got a job offer to move to L.A. she talked me into relocating here from Atlanta. At first I thought she was crazy to even suggest a thing. Why would I want to leave Hot-Lanta for docile D.C.? But I came and stayed a week and fell in love with the area. Then I knew I had to live here. And I fell in love with the house. I thought it was just what I needed, real nice although at times I think it's way too big for a bachelor. I ended up convincing her to sell it to me."

She bet his house was nice. Too bad she probably would never get to see it. "I need to apologize to you, Lucien," she said, deciding not to put off saying what she needed to say any longer. Besides, that was the reason he'd brought her here. "I'm usually more together than that. I didn't mean to start crying earlier today."

"It's okay. You were frustrated and needed to let it out. It can happen to the best of us."

"Yes, but—"

"But nothing, Jaclyn," he said softly. "I can understand your frustration. I don't know what the Matthewses are trying to prove by filing that lawsuit. The hospital will suffer unnecessarily when what they should be doing is getting their son the help he needs. Denying that Terrence has a problem isn't helping the situation or him."

"But what if their attorneys demand to know who told you about Terrence?"

"Like I told you, they can't force us to give them the information. And as far as the staff trying to figure out who told, sounds to me they have too much time on their hands. But realistically, there's no way to stop them from talking. Your secret is safe."

She certainly hoped so. They refrained from talking when the waitress returned with their food and set the plates in front of them. She hadn't known the omelet was so huge and told Lucien so.

He lifted an amused brow. "Didn't you know that George was an important man in this town? Anything representing him can only be big."

"Then explain the dollar bill, Lucien."

With a very serious expression he said, "It was a lost bet. I understand that George and good ole Ben Franklin tossed coins to see who would get top dibs and George lost."

Jaclyn couldn't help but laugh. It felt good to laugh and it felt good, for whatever the reason, to be sharing breakfast with the man she had fallen in love with. If anyone saw them it would appear as if they were on a breakfast date. But she knew they were not on a date. They were just colleagues sharing coffee and a meal.

"So, do you get to go home often?" she asked him, trying not to notice how his mouth moved while he chewed his food. There was something downright sexy about it. He waited until after he swallowed his food to respond.

"Not as much as I would like, and my grandmother and sister remind me of that every time we talk. Because of my work at the hospital, I haven't been home in two years. I plan to go to Kingston for the holidays, though."

"I bet that will be nice."

Lucien nodded slowly as he sipped his coffee. "Yes, it will be and it will get my sister off my back for a while."

"The two of you are close?"

"Yes, very. My grandmother raised me and my sister, as well as two of our cousins. We're all close. My sister Lori is a practicing attorney in L.A. My cousin Martie is a surgeon in Seattle and my other cousin Danielle is an accountant in New York."

"All of you are spread out," she noted.

His mouth curved in a smile. "Yes, but we enjoy traveling to visit each other when we can get together. The four of us became naturalized citizens our second year in college, but we still consider Jamaica home."

"I bet it's beautiful."

"It is."

He'd said it in a voice filled with love for the place where he was born. He might be a citizen of the United States now, but she could tell Jamaica was a part of his heart.

The waitress materialized to clear away their plates and to see if they wanted more coffee, and because

Jaclyn was enjoying their conversations and he hadn't shown an inclination to leave just yet, they had refills.

"You worked up an appetite during the past eighteen hours, so if you're still hungry we can order you another George Washington," he said over the rim of his cup as he took another sip of coffee.

"You got to be kidding. If I eat another omelet you'll have to roll me out of here," she said chuckling. "I should not have eaten all of that. Now instead of going home and going straight to bed I'm going to have to find some physical activities to get into."

"And what kind of physical activities do you think you might be interested in, Jaclyn?" he asked silkily.

The words flowed across her skin like a physical caress and her nipples suddenly felt tight and erect. She didn't have to glance down at her chest to know they were probably poking through her blouse, a telltale sign that she'd gotten aroused by his question.

He proved that point when his gaze slowly moved from her face to shift downward. She quickly picked up her coffee cup to hold it in front of her, trying to act natural, but from the look in his eyes, she knew she'd failed. She couldn't help but shiver under the intensity of his gaze.

His eyes then returned to hers. "There is something else I think we need to discuss, Jaclyn," he said in a voice so low and sexy that it seemed to rumble out each and every syllable.

"And what is that?" she asked thinking the coffee was only making her feel hotter. She needed something cold like lemonade or iced tea to cool her off.

He continued to hold her gaze and she felt her pulse rate increase when he said, "The kiss that almost happened in my office yesterday."

Her mouth instantly dried and she struggled to swallow. She'd hoped he had forgotten about that. But there was no reason for her to deny it when she'd known the moment had been real. Had the 911 alert not gone off, they would have shared a kiss and they both knew it. If he could own up to it, then so could she.

"I need to apologize for that, too," she said softly.

"Why?"

His question surprised her. "Because I'm the one who called the meeting and I'm the one who let it get out of hand. The only reason you were comforting me was because I broke down in tears."

Lucien had been listening to her with his cup halfway to his lips. "Yes and no." He set down his cup.

She raised a brow. "Yes and no? What do you mean?"

"It's true you called the meeting, but I'm the one who made the move to hold you in my arms."

"Because I was crying," she said.

His gaze darkened with a heat she felt in every bone in her body. "Because I wanted to hold you," he corrected.

Her nipples acted up again and felt achy as they rubbed against both her bra and blouse. And even worse, when his gaze shifted to her mouth, she felt tingling sensations in her lips. Was he saying what she thought he was saying? Was he admitting that he'd held her not because she was crying but because he'd wanted to?

She must have had a confused look on her face because he then said, "I just wanted to clear that up."

She shook her head. If he honestly thought he'd cleared anything up, he was sadly mistaken. He'd only opened up a can of worms. Maybe this wasn't the time or the place to ask, but he had brought it up. "Lucien, why would you want to hold me?" she asked in a whispered voice. The café was a lot more crowded now than when they'd first arrived, filling up with students and workers who needed a cup of coffee and breakfast to kick-start their day.

He glanced around and noticed the crowd. When he looked back at her a smile played around his lips. That same smile played her insides like a string guitar. And his dark eyes had latched on to hers, almost making breathing difficult. "Let's go and finish this discussion someplace else," he suggested.

She nodded. Would he invite her to his home? He did say he lived in the area. But no, that wouldn't be right. Being alone in his office was one thing, but she had no reason to visit his home. "Someplace like where?" she heard herself asking.

"I know it's still early, but there's a nice park nearby. The Georgetown Waterfront Park. I go there a lot when I need some me time."

Jaclyn thought it was good to know others needed alone time as well. She was definitely a stickler for it. Spending so much time in the hospital, tending to the physical and sometimes emotional needs of the patients could be somewhat draining and made her appreciate solitude. There was nothing like getting away for a few quiet moments.

"So will you go there with me, Jaclyn? If you prefer not to, I'd understand. You pulled a double shift yesterday."

Yes, she had and so had he. There was something about being here with him that had her adrenaline flowing, and she wasn't ready to put a cap on it. She smiled at him and said, "Yes, I'd love to go to the park with you."

Chapter 5

Lucien knew he had no business spending time with Jaclyn Campbell, let along asking her to spend time at the park with him. What in the world was he thinking?

He drew in a deep breath as he put the key in his car's ignition, knowing just what he'd been thinking. How good she'd looked sitting across from him, with her creamy smooth skin, gorgeous hazel eyes and chin-length straight brown hair. And how good she'd looked when he'd seen her about to leave the hospital in a pair of khakis and a pretty pink blouse. But most of all he'd thought about making nights of endless love to that lush body of hers.

He came to a stop at an intersection in the H Street Corridor and glanced over at her. He couldn't help remembering the moment she had become aroused by something he'd said. Her body had responded right before his eyes. He had just finished asking her what kind of physical activities she might be interested in. He wondered if her mind had followed the path his had taken. The thought of that possibility gave him some wicked pleasure he shouldn't be experiencing.

What was it going to take to make him think rationally where she was concerned? He should be thinking with the head connected to his neck and not the other head that throbbed each and every time he glanced over at her.

"It's going to be a beautiful day."

He glanced over at her, finding it hard not to say that the beauty of his day had begun with her. The moment he'd seen her about to leave the hospital he was pushed into motion to do something. The E.R. situation had kept him busy, focused and concentrated on saving lives. But when he'd taken a moment to breathe when all the injured patients had been cared for, his gaze had immediately sought her out. She had been busy suturing a cut on a man's forehead, concentrating intently on her patient. He hadn't been surprised. When it came to taking care of those who came to Hopewell General, she was always on top of her game.

"Yes, it is." He smiled. "A great day to have a boat race."

She lifted a brow. "A boat race?"

His smile widened. "Yes, but relax. I'm talking about remote-operated toy boats. A friend of mine and I like putting them in the pond at the park to see who is king of the waterways."

"And you have these boats with you?"

He chuckled. "Just so happens that I do. Both his and mine are in the trunk. I'm sure he'll feel that any woman who knows anything about what's under the hood of car is entitled to use his boat. So what do you say, Jaclyn?"

Jaclyn couldn't help but return Lucien's smile. He'd conveniently forgotten that they were supposed to be discussing the kiss they'd almost shared in his office yesterday. Evidently he wasn't ready to go there again just yet, so she would indulge him for the moment.

"Should I warn you that in addition to being an auto mechanic, my father loves boats as well? I did mention he bought one a few years ago and taught me how to operate it."

He parked the car in the park and glanced over at her as if he was sizing up the competition. "Should I remind you we're talking about toy boats?" he asked, clearly amused.

"And just for the record," he added. "Maybe I should also remind you that I came from a place literally sur-rounded by water. Knowing how to swim and how to operate a boat were a must-do. In fact I worked on a boat dock from the time I was fourteen. I saved my money to apply for college in America."

"Impressive. So this friend of yours whose boat I'll be using, are you sure he won't mind?"

"If he thought for one minute you'd use it to beat me, then I can tell you he won't. And you happen to know him."

She lifted a brow. "I do?"

"Yes. Dr. Thomas Bradshaw."

She nodded. There wasn't a person at Hopewell who didn't know Dr. Bradshaw. A pure workaholic if ever there was one, he was the youngest person ever to be named head of surgery at Hopewell. That made him the envy of a number of other surgeons. And she'd heard he was as arrogant as he was handsome. On the other hand, in comparison, she thought Lucien didn't have an arrogant bone in his body. They were like day and night.

"Dr. Bradshaw is a close friend of yours?" she asked surprised.

He chuckled. "Yes. Why do you find that hard to believe?"

Jaclyn would rather not say. She could see him and Dr. Bradshaw being colleagues. But close friends? Friends who would share time racing toy boats? "No reason. Okay, Lucien, bring on the race."

There was something about Georgetown Waterfront Park that reminded Lucien of parts of Kingston. Maybe it was the way the waterways stretched from one harbor to the other, or the flowering trees that lined the boardwalk.

"Will we be racing our boats in the river?" Jaclyn asked, pulling his thoughts back to her, not that they'd fully ever left. The wind was blowing and her hair was like silk fanning around her face.

"No, there's a small pond on the other side that will be perfect," he said, taking the boats out of the trunk of his car. She was standing beside him looking on and he thought she smelled good, definitely not like someone who'd pulled a double shift.

"This one is yours," he said, handing her a twenty-eight-inch toy replica of a speed boat.

She took it and their hands touched. He had the same reaction that he had the other day when he'd handed her back the charts. Their gazes met and he felt a heat flow through him. He was aware of the intense ache in the lower part of his body and decided to pause a moment. Inhale and exhale. He did so while desire coursed through his veins in a way it had never done before.

"Let me see the boat you'll be using, Lucien."

The sound of her voice invaded some outcropped part of his brain, made him realize he needed to get a grip. He hadn't explained why he had wanted to kiss her yesterday and already he was fighting the urge to kiss her again. He knew she was probably aware of it and was trying to bring him back around. Let reality invade.

Taking another deep breath he pulled his own boat out of the trunk. "So what do you think?" he asked, showing it to her.

She smiled up at him. "It's cute, but I like mine better."

"Cute? Hey, you won't be saying that in a little while," he said, closing down the trunk and trying to force back the desire he felt just from her smile.

She shrugged. "We'll see." And without saying anything else she fell into step beside him.

At that moment her presence next to him felt right.

* * *

She liked walking beside him, Jaclyn thought as they made their way to the pond. She didn't want to think of the way he had looked at her a few minutes ago. It was the same way he had looked at her yesterday after she'd dropped those charts on the floor and he'd help her gather them up. The same way he'd looked at her just before he'd almost kissed her. The same way he'd looked at her at the café.

He led her over toward a grassy bank. It was a small pond surrounded by flowering plants off the side of a boardwalk. "I hope the ducks and geese don't mind sharing today," she said when she saw how many were in the pond.

"Once we put the boats in the water and start them up, the birds will start scattering."

Jaclyn glanced over at him. "You sure?"

"It happens each and every time."

Moments later after they set their boats in the water, the first sound of the humming from the boats sent the geese and ducks flying. "Do you ever feel as if you're invading their turf?" she asked him.

He chuckled. "Not at all. They have the entire sky, so they should not mind if we use their water." He then said, "The rules of the game are simple. The first boat to the other side wins."

A smile curving her lips was her only response.

He hunched down and set the boats next to each other and she knelt down beside him with her remote in her hand. "On your mark…get set…go."

The boats took off and at some point they were even

as they crossed the pond. But then suddenly hers took the lead. He glanced over at her, saw the smirk of victory on her face. "I wouldn't get cocky so soon." And then suddenly, his boat took the lead. They stood there, cheering their boats on. In the end his boat made it to the other side first.

He glanced over at her smiling. "Well, what do you think?"

"My mom was right."

"About what?"

"Men are boys who like playing with more expensive toys."

He threw his head back and laughed. "You're going to be a sore loser?"

"No, but you do know I want another race."

"I think I can accommodate you."

It took a few minutes to get the boats back to their side of the pond to start the race up again. She won the next one and he took the lead, winning the next two. "We've raced our boats enough for today. Let's sit down and talk," he said, gesturing to a bench that faced the pond.

"All right."

There weren't a lot of people about and the geese and ducks, Jaclyn noticed, flew back the moment they'd taken the boats out of the pond. It was a beautiful day in August and numerous boats could be seen out on the Potomac.

He sat beside her and they didn't say anything for a few moments. She knew they were both enmeshed deep in their own thoughts. Moments later, his soft chuckle drew her attention.

"What's so amusing?"

"You. Me. The boat race," he said, stretching out his legs. "When we left the hospital this morning after pulling a double, you should have gone to your place and I should have gone to mine."

Jaclyn nodded slowly. "Why didn't we?"

A grim smile curved the corners of his mouth. "That would have been way too easy. Besides, we needed to talk."

And it was a conversation they still hadn't had, at least not fully. "Okay, Lucien, let's talk."

Silence lingered between them for a moment .Then he said, "The reason I almost kissed you in my office yesterday was because I wanted to kiss you. It had nothing to do with your tears, although they provided the perfect opportunity, an advantage I didn't waste any time taking."

Jaclyn made no reply. All she could do at the moment was to listen while her body responded to the husky sound of his voice.

"And the reason I wanted to kiss you," he continued to say, "is that in case you hadn't noticed, I'm attracted to you."

He hesitated, as if he expected her to make a comment and when she didn't, he said, "And being attracted to you isn't a good thing considering the hospital's policy and your position and mine."

She looked down for a few moments and then looked back at him. She saw the intensity in his eyes and thought it was time she said something. It was time for her to let him know the attraction was not one-sided. "I'm attracted to you as well, Lucien."

She decided it was best not to let him know her feelings had moved from mere attraction to love. There were still a lot of things she didn't know about him, but it didn't matter. At least not to her heart.

She loved him.

She swallowed hard when she saw the impact her confession had on him. It was there in his features, in the way the muscles tightened in his jaw, the way the pupils of his eyes darkened even more. "Had I met you at a medical convention, research seminar or just passing by on the street, I would welcome the attraction. But considering the hospital's policy… Well, it is what it is."

"Yes, it is what it is," he agreed slowly in a husky tone.

She hesitated a moment and then said, "I know you aren't married. At least the word among the interns is that you're not. But are you involved with anyone?"

A smile curved his lips. "No. I haven't been seriously involved with anyone for close to a year. In fact I haven't dated anyone since October of last year."

She wondered if he'd intentionally told her that period of time because it was when she'd begun working at the hospital. Was it his way of letting her know he hadn't dated a woman since they'd met?

"What about you, Jaclyn? Is there some serious guy in your life?"

She tried not to frown when she thought about

Danny, the guy she had dated seriously while in her first year of med school. She could clearly remember when he had graduated from law school and had accompanied a group of friends to England for a summer vacation well-earned. Jaclyn couldn't forget how he had returned to the States and dropped by to see her just long enough to break things off with her. He had explained he had met someone in London and it had been love at first sight.

At the time she had been too hurt to consider that such a thing was possible, but now after meeting Lucien, she knew better and could appreciate Danny for not stringing her along. Instead, he had followed his heart. According to her brother who still heard from Danny from time to time, he went back to London, married the woman he loved and the two were now living in Rhode Island where Danny was working at a law firm and was the father of a little girl.

She glanced over at Lucien and saw he was waiting for her response. "No, I'm not seeing anyone seriously. At least not now. My boyfriend and I broke up a little over a year ago and I've been too busy to become involved in another serious relationship."

What she didn't add was that even if she hadn't been busy she probably would have not become involved again. She had put a lot of time into her relationship with Danny and in the end he'd still walked…right into the arms of another woman.

"What about Marcus Shaw? He seems to like you."

Was that a tinge of jealousy she heard in his voice? She shook her head, finding the notion ridiculous, especially when she thought of the playboy intern. "Marcus likes to flirt with all the ladies. If you notice I never flirt back."

He nodded. "No, you don't." Then he stood, held out his hand to her and said, "Come take a walk with me."

"What about our boats?" she asked.

"We can leave them here for a minute."

The moment she placed her hand in his, she felt it. A tingling sensation all the way to her toes. Suddenly his hand tightened on hers in what seemed to be a possessive grip as she stood on her feet while forcing the cozy awareness from her mind. Standing up brought them so close that there was barely any breathing space between them. Up close she could only marvel at the breadth of his wide shoulders and powerful chest, and a face that could make a woman drool.

"Ready?" He leaned over and whispered close to her ear.

She swallowed and wondered what she was supposed to be ready for. "Yes."

His hand continued to hold hers as they began walking along a grassy path that led away from the pond toward an area shrouded by huge cherry blossoms and magnolia trees. The area would be perfect for a picnic with the lush lawns and the Potomac River as a backdrop.

He stopped at a huge maple tree and he perched his back against the bark. She followed his line of vision and saw he had a good view of where they'd left the boats. And then his gaze moved over her features. "Do you know what I thought when I first saw you?" he asked her.

She smiled. "Probably the same thing you thought of all the other interns. That we had a lot to learn before we could call ourselves doctors."

He chuckled. "Yes, that too, but I'm talking about when I first saw you specifically. You might not have noticed, but my gaze stayed on you a minute too long."

She had noticed but assumed she had imagined it because her gaze had remained on him even longer than that. "No, I didn't know what you were thinking," she whispered when she realized just how close they were standing.

"I thought you were more than just pretty. I thought you were strikingly beautiful, which is something I should not have been thinking. I also thought, less than a few minutes later, that with you I was going to have to keep my distance. I had immediately felt an attraction to you and I knew that was not going to work."

"Is that why you transferred me to nights for a while?" she decided to ask him.

"Yes," he responded honestly. "That, and I thought the E.R. could use a person like you. You have a way with patients. You have a lot of patience."

With some things, she thought, knowing her patience was being stretched at this very moment. They were talking, true enough. And he had admitted to being attracted to her. But he hadn't explained what had made the attraction so great he'd been willing to risk breaking a hospital policy by kissing her.

"I can't explain it, Jaclyn," he said softly, as if he'd

read her mind. "Nor do I fully understand it. All I know is that at that moment, I had to taste you." Then in an even lower voice he added, "I had to know the sweetness of your mouth, and how your tongue would feel wrapped around mine, with me sucking on it, devouring it."

Whatever she'd assumed he would eventually get around to saying, that wasn't it. His words made her heart start racing in her chest at the same time that her breath caught in her throat. Luscious and succulent images filled her mind while sensations crammed her body in a heated rush. She could feel her eyes darken as she watched his do likewise. And then of its own accord, her body leaned into him and his head lowered and swooped down on her mouth to finish what they'd started before the interruption yesterday.

It had to be the most focused kiss she'd ever experienced. It seemed he was putting everything into it. His every thought, all five senses and a flood of emotions. And when she felt his arms wrap around her, she automatically sank into him. At that moment she couldn't think and was relying on him to do all the thinking for both of them. All she could do was give herself over to a kiss she was feeling all the way to her toes.

Lucien felt his mind and body unleash turbulent emotions that he'd held back for the past eighteen months. Now he was giving in to a hunger he hadn't known possible. There was this ravenousness that was invading his body and obliterating any kind of control. And he was giving in to it. Letting it dominate.

Her tongue tasted just as he'd known it would with a sweetness that was turning his bones to jelly. There was a faint taste of the spiced coffee she'd drunk earlier, but mostly it was all woman and it was so captivating that he couldn't imagine how it would be not to kiss her.

He pushed that thought out of his mind as he continued to devour her mouth, lips, tongue. There wasn't a part of her mouth he hadn't invaded and sampled. And she was kissing him back with a hunger just as greedy as his own.

The sound of people approaching had them breaking off the kiss, but Lucien was intent on feasting on her mouth anyway and began licking the corners of her lips, tracing the outline with the tip of his tongue, leaving a wet trail from corner to corner. And when she moaned the word "Oh" and her mouth formed into the shape of a bow, he licked around that as well.

When the voices came closer his hold around her waist loosened and he shifted slightly while taking a step back. Their gazes held while a couple with a child walked past. Lucien had a gut feeling when reality returned they would realize just what line they had crossed. They were treading on forbidden ground, but he needed her to know he wasn't remorseful in any way.

"I don't regret kissing you, Jaclyn," he said. "This was personal and our relationship at the hospital is business. I can separate the two." But he knew the officials at the hospital wouldn't agree, which was why they had the nonfraternization policy in place.

"And just so we're absolutely clear about something. I'm not a boss who makes it a point to hit on one intern out of every group I get. Nothing like this has ever happened to me before. You are the one and only woman I've been this attracted to." He hoped she knew that he was being completely honestly with her because he was.

"And nothing like this has ever happened to me before. I didn't intentionally set out to draw your attention either," she said.

He believed her. Like he'd said earlier, there were some things that were hard to deny and for him it was an attraction of this magnitude. He leaned in and kissed her again. He couldn't help it. It seemed her lips had parted just for him.

This kiss was gentler than the first but just as ravenous on both their parts. He didn't just want to kiss her, he wanted to lay claim to every inch of her mouth and he was doing so inch by inch and second by second.

The sweetness of her mouth was holding him captive and he surrendered easily with a hunger he couldn't deny. But when a plane flew overhead the noise nearly causing the ground beneath them to vibrate, he accepted that as his cue to release her mouth.

"You can become habit-forming," he whispered against her moist lips.

"If only things could be that easy," was her quick response and he knew exactly what she'd meant. They'd crossed over to forbidden grounds and weren't sure how to go back. Things wouldn't be easy between them from now on, no matter what route they chose to take.

He saw the desire in her eyes and he saw something else, too. Weariness. She had to be tired. "Come on," he said, taking a step back and reclaiming her hand.

"I'm taking you home." Her hand felt so right enclosed in his.

She glanced up at him when they began walking back toward the area where they'd left their boats. "You mean you're taking me back to the hospital for my car, don't you?"

"No, I'm taking you home. You're exhausted." When she parted her lips to protest, he quickly said, "Don't argue about it, Jaclyn. If you need me to take you to get your car tomorrow I can do that."

"That won't be necessary. My roommate can take me to get it later today."

They gathered the boats with the remotes and walked back to the car. She had gotten silent on him and was probably wondering where their kiss would lead. He had no answer to that question. They didn't even have the luxury of taking things one day at a time. Whatever was going on between them needed to end now. But he couldn't make himself do that.

When they were in the car with seat belts in place, he decided to engage in conversation about anything and everything but the kiss they'd shared. They talked about recent movies they'd seen, mostly on DVD, because their time was limited when it came to going to the theaters. He wasn't surprised that they enjoyed the same movies and actors. It should have been a simple matter to ask her out on a movie date, but he knew doing something like that was only asking for trouble.

He didn't know about her, but he considered their day in the park as a date and the thought that it would be the only one they could have made sadness well up inside of him. The one thing he wanted—a relationship with her—was the one thing he could not have.

Once he crossed the Francis Scott Key Bridge, it didn't take them long to reach where she lived. She had given him good directions. He brought his car to a stop in front of a nicely landscaped town house. "Nice place."

"Thanks. It's owned by friends of my parents who spend most of their time out of the country since retiring. They offered me the use of it. I have a roommate to defray the cost because it's in a nice part of town."

He nodded. "Dr. Morales is your roommate, right?"

"Yes, that's right."

He figured the reason she wouldn't be inviting him in was because Dr. Morales would have come home from the hospital by now. Chances were she was sleeping off the long hours spent at the hospital because she'd stayed on duty most of the night. That was a risk neither of them needed to take.

"Thanks for such a fun day, Lucien. I had a wonderful time…even if you did best me three out of four on the boat race."

He smiled. "There's always another time, Jaclyn."

He wasn't sure why he was putting ideas into her head that they could spend another day together when they both knew they couldn't. They had too much to lose. He had the position he wanted at the hospital and she had her entire future as a doctor to protect.

Instead of responding to what he'd said, she proceeded to unbuckle her seat belt. When he began unbuckling his, she glanced over at him and asked, "What are you doing?"

"Walking you to the door."

She nervously gnawed on her bottom lip. "You don't have to do that."

"Yes, I do." He had to do it for more reasons than one. Most importantly because this was probably the last date, official or otherwise, they would ever share. And although he figured they both had to be exhausted, he wasn't ready for their day together to end.

He waited to see if she would present some sort of argument and gave a sigh of relief when she didn't. Together they disembarked the car and began walking toward her front door.

Upon reaching their destination, she pulled the key from her purse and glanced up at him. "I would invite you in, but my—"

"Yes, I know. More than likely Dr. Morales is home," he finished for her.

Her mouth curved in a slight smile. "Yes."

He slanted her a smile. "I'll see you back at the hospital but no sooner than Friday. If I recall, you have the next two days off."

"Only if they don't need me."

"They won't. You deserve to get some rest. Got that?"

She chuckled. "Yes, I got that. And you don't have to worry about me showing up before then," she said. "After I take a shower I'll probably fall face down in my bed and sleep for the next forty-eight hours."

A sudden vision jerked his brain to life—that of her

stepping out of the shower, naked, with water glisten-
ing all over her body. The thought had goose bumps
prickling his skin while blood rushed fast and furious
through his veins.

"I'll be seeing you, then," she said, and made a move
to open the door.

"Yes, I'll be seeing you."

He turned to leave and had even taken a few steps.
But something made him turn back toward her. All it
took was a look in her eyes and he was a goner. Without any thought he retraced his steps to her and pulled
her into his arms. She parted her lips invitingly.

The moment his tongue touched hers, like before,
passion ripped through him and he deepened the kiss
as hunger took control. For all he knew her roommate
could have been standing at the window staring at them,
but for the moment he didn't care. The only thing he
cared about was kissing her, tasting her, claiming her
mouth this way once again.

Never had he found kissing a woman so deep-in-
the-gut pleasurable. Never had he been so caught up
in a kiss. Her lips were soft and pliable; her tongue
was just as aggressive and greedy as his. He detected a
need within her that was just as great as his own. So he
deepened the kiss, continued a thorough sweep around
the insides of her mouth like he had all the time in the
world. He was taking it whether he had it or not.

She was the one who pulled away from the kiss to
gasp for air. And as he watched her battle short breaths,
a tiny voice inside his head scolded that he should not

have kissed her again. But he knew there was no way he could have left without doing so.

He slowly ran his tongue around the upper part of his lips, enjoying the taste of her still lingering there. He reached out and gently rubbed the pad of his thumb across her chin wondering what he could say to free himself from a moment that would forever be trapped in his mind. And he knew there was nothing he would say. "I'll be seeing you."

She nodded. "All right."

Forcing distance between them he turned and jogged back to his car. One thought rang in his mind: What had he gotten himself into?

Chapter 6

Jaclyn took a shower and fell into bed. The moment her head touched the pillow she should have been fast asleep. But that was not the case. Her lips were still tingling and her body was still keyed up from the kiss she had shared with Lucien.

They hadn't kissed just once but twice, not counting the nibbles in between as well as the encore at her door. She could definitely say her mouth had gotten quite a workout. She had never been kissed so soundly by a man in her life. He hadn't just kissed her, he had literally consumed her.

The one thing she had been grateful for was that Isabelle had slept through it all. That meant her friend and roommate knew nothing about the sensuous exchange on their doorstep. She was also relieved that as far as she knew, no other employee of the hospital lived in their neighborhood.

She had two days off and hopefully by the time she returned to work she would be on solid ground, ready to put the time she'd spent with Lucien behind her.

Fat chance!

She changed positions on the bed wondering if counting sheep would help and quickly figured that it wouldn't. So she flipped on her back and stared at the ceiling to think. How was she supposed to act when she saw him again? How could she manage to look at him, gaze at his mouth and not remember how that same mouth had wiped all her senses clean with a smooth stroke of his tongue?

And they had been the smoothest strokes, with such thorough possession that she got butterflies in her stomach at the mere memory. Just like the interns referred to Ms. Tsang as "Miss Thang" behind her back, a few of the interns had taken to calling Dr. De Winter "De Man" behind his back. Well, he had shown her today that he was definitely *the* man.

She was about to close her eyes when her cell phone went off and she quickly recognized the ring tone. It was one or both of her parents. She quickly picked it up. The last time one of them called was to tell her that her grandmother had taken a fall. "Hello?"

"Hi, precious. How's my favorite girl?"

Jaclyn smiled. She and her father always had a close relationship. She wasn't ashamed to admit she was a daddy's girl. "I'm fine, Dad. How're you, Mom and Gramma doing?"

Jaclyn's grandfather had died the year she had started medical school. Childhood sweethearts, her grandparents had been married over sixty years. After he died, everyone had wondered how her grandmother would handle the loneliness. But Gloria Campbell had surprised everyone by joining a senior citizens' club where the over-seventy group did a number of activities each day.

"Everyone is fine. We heard about that multicar pileup on CNN. A reporter said all the injured people were taken to the hospital where you work."

"Yes, that's right. I had to pull a double."

She and her father talked a little while longer before he passed the phone to her mother. Hearing the exhaustion in her voice, her mother gave her instructions to get rest, told her that her grandmother was at the senior citizens' center playing bingo and then ended the call.

They were great parents, Jaclyn thought as she hung up the phone. She couldn't imagine growing up without them, and her brother.

Kevin had always been a clean-cut kid until he went away to college. It was there when he began experimenting with drugs and eventually got addicted. He had returned home in his junior year of college with a drug habit. A year later her parents had to Baker Act him when his illegal drug use had gotten out of control. It had taken some time, but with the family's support he had pulled himself together, gone back to finish college and met and married a wonderful woman. Trish was just the person her brother had needed in his life.

She wouldn't be surprised if Kevin called her as well

to check up on her. Although she would love hearing from him she needed to sleep and hoped her parents passed the word that she was fine and just needed to rest.

Kevin would be the first to tell anyone that upon admitting he'd had a drug problem the best thing he'd gotten was support from his family.

That was why she found the Matthewses' lawsuit so confusing. Terrence had a drug problem and the worst thing his parents could do was stick their heads in the sand and pretend that he didn't. He needed help, and with the right type of counseling there was no doubt in her mind that Terrence would one day become the gifted physician she believed he could be. But the route his parents were taking was one of denial. They were going after the hospital for revenge. It didn't make any sense.

Jaclyn shifted positions in bed and her thoughts moved from Terrence back to Lucien. She didn't want to face the fact that today she had gotten her first and last kisses from him. As she closed her eyes and drifted off to sleep she still had the taste of Lucien on her tongue. And she liked it. She liked it too much.

Lucien left his bedroom in his bare feet and walked to the kitchen to grab a beer out of the refrigerator. He popped the bottle cap and took a huge pleasurable gulp. What a day, he thought. What a woman. What a kiss.

Before coming home he had gone back to the hospital to check on the patients who had been brought in through E.R. yesterday. He hadn't run into Dr. Dudley, but he had seen Nurse Tsang, who had locked her gaze on him like she'd known he was hiding something. He couldn't help but smile. If only she knew… And he was so damn grateful that she didn't. It was bad enough that he did.

He rubbed his hand down his face thinking of the predicament he was in. But instead of trying to come up with a way out of it, his mind was conjuring a plan to get further into forbidden territory. It made no sense. First and foremost he was Jaclyn's boss, which meant he had no right dating her even if the hospital didn't have a policy against it.

He dropped down in a chair at the kitchen table remembering the last time he'd gotten involved in a workplace relationship and how badly it had ended. What he'd told Jaclyn was true. He wasn't involved with anyone and hadn't been seriously in quite a while. He'd also been honest when he'd said he'd never been involved with an intern under his supervision.

But what he hadn't told her was that years ago when he had been a intern himself he'd dated another med student by the name of Nikki Stinson. Both he and Nikki were very competitive and when he earned a better intern placement than she did, the affair ended badly. That was when he'd decided never to mix business with pleasure again. So why was he so into Jaclyn? Not only was he breaking the hospital rule, but he was also breaking his own rule.

Granted, Jaclyn was nothing like Nikki. Nikki had grown up in the Bronx and was tough as nails. There were times he thought there wasn't a compassionate bone in her body, which made him question her choice of profession. More than once Nikki's bedside demeanor with patients had been so atrocious that she had gotten written up by their superiors. Jaclyn, on the other hand, had a gentle, calm nature, a kindness that gave him the impression she was emotionally fragile. Not weak but vulnerable. She had a way of bringing out the very essence of his protective instincts.

A short while later, even though it was still daylight outside, Lucien was in his bed lying flat on his back and staring up at the ceiling. He had truly enjoyed spending the day with Jaclyn. When he'd mentioned the boat race, she hadn't given him a funny look or made a wisecrack about a grown man who would like doing such a thing. Instead, she had smiled and joined in an activity that he enjoyed, one that always relaxed him.

Being around her had relaxed him as well. She was the type of woman a man could open up to, the kind of woman a man could get attached to if he wasn't careful. He drew in a deep breath. Who was he kidding? He was already a goner. If he was smart he would put Jaclyn and the kisses they'd shared not only to the back of his mind but out of his mind completely. But for some reason he couldn't do that.

When he'd kissed her he had been caught off guard by how delicious she tasted. Intense heat had circulated in his stomach and moved lower to his groin. It had filled him with desire so thick and potent that he'd succumbed to the very power of it by deepening the kiss. He hadn't experienced anything so erotic in his entire life.

Lucien knew he had felt every luscious curve of her body when he had held her close to him. It had been a beautiful day and he had been lucky enough to hold a beautiful woman in his arms. But he had done more than just hold her. He had kissed her with a possession that he'd felt all through his body. And the strange thing about it was that he still felt it.

And when she had shivered in his arms, he had felt each and every vibration in a way that made his gut rumble with need that has been so urgent and vital that his pulse rate had raced out of control. His mind had suddenly filled with possibilities of just how far that kiss could take him, and he'd known it would be beyond anything in his wildest dreams. In other words, each kiss had shaken him to the very core of his being.

Even now his pulse was accelerating just remembering their day together. A day he hadn't wanted to end. He was surprised he had won the race those four times because he hadn't been able to take his eyes off her. The sun had been shining bright in the sky and the rays had hit her at an angle that had made her look gorgeous from the top of her head to the soles of her feet.

He couldn't help wondering what she would be doing with her free time over the next two days. He hadn't mentioned it to her but he had the next two days off work as well. Imagine that. He drew in a deep breath, not wanting to imagine it. If they had been free to date he would call her in a heartbeat and suggest they spend their days off together.

But they weren't free to date and that was the crux of his problem. He knew the limitations, the boundaries and the risks, yet today he had outright ignored all three and today he had done just what he'd wanted to do where Jaclyn was concerned. And a part of him knew tomorrow wasn't going to be any better. Already he was contemplating calling her and asking that they spend their two days off together. Now if that wasn't asking for trouble, what was?

Doing something like that would be the most irrational thing he'd ever done. However, at the moment he wasn't strong enough to resist her. He wanted to see her again, spend time with her and taste her once more.

Before he could talk himself out of doing it, he reached for his cell phone on the nightstand. He had every intern's number in his phone and the moment he punched in her name he could hear the ringing sound.

What if he was waking her up from a sound sleep? She had mentioned she planned on going straight to bed after taking a shower. Just because he was too wired to sleep didn't mean she was, too. On the third ring he'd made up his mind to hang up when she answered the call.

"Hello?"

His heart slammed in his chest at the sexy, husky and sluggish sound of her voice. He had awakened her, but damn, she sounded so good. That same pulse that had been giving him fits all day began to thud almost mercilessly in his chest. He was so caught up in how she sounded that it was only when she said hello a second time that he realized he needed to say something. His reaction to her wasn't normal, but for him normalcy had gotten tossed to the wind the moment he'd laid his eyes on Jaclyn that day at Hopewell.

He closed his eyes and then reopened them, knowing what he was about to ask would change the course of their relationship forever. "This is Lucien. Sorry if I woke you, but I need to ask you something."

"What?"

He decided to jump right in. The worst she could do was tell him no. "I'm off work the next two days as well. I plan to get away and go sailing on the Chesapeake and wanted to know if you'll go with me."

And just so she understood the depth of what he was asking, he quickly added, "And I'd like to make it an overnight trip, so we won't be returning until sometime Thursday."

Jaclyn jolted wide awake. Had she dreamed what Lucien had just said? What he'd suggested? "Sorry, could you repeat that? I think I misunderstood you."

His soft chuckle sent heat flowing through her body and her lips suddenly felt dry, so she licked them. "I'm asking you to spend two days with me. I'd like for us to take a drive over to Annapolis, then spend the day sailing on the Chesapeake. I know the perfect place where we can stay for the night."

She swallowed thickly. After two kisses did he just assume she would sleep with him? She sat up at the edge of the bed. Don't jump to any conclusions, she told herself. All he'd said was that he wanted her to spend the day with him tomorrow. He hadn't come right out and said they would be sharing a bed. He would expect them to get separate rooms, wouldn't he?

"Jaclyn?"

"Yes?"

"We can get separate rooms, if you'd like."

She wondered if he had read her thoughts. She hadn't missed the way he'd made the suggestion. He would leave it up to her to decide whether there would be one room or two.

"Will you spend your off days with me?" he asked when moments slipped by and she hadn't said anything.

She began nibbling on her bottom lip. He sounded as if he was in his right mind, which meant he was well aware of the risks if they were seen together, regardless of the sleeping arrangements. "Lucien…"

"I know what you're thinking and yes, I know the risks. I knew them today as well. But that didn't keep me from wanting you, wanting to hold you in my arms and kiss you. And knowing the risks isn't keeping me from wanting to spend the next two days with you. I know it's crazy, but I want to be with you."

Jaclyn inhaled slowly. If it was crazy, then he wasn't the only one affected by this madness because she wanted to spend time with him as well. For the past eighteen months they had shared an intense attraction but had resorted to pretending the other hadn't existed. At least they had tried to pretend. But for the next two days he was giving her a chance not to pretend and by golly she would take it. "What time will you pick me up?"

He didn't say anything for a second, as if surprised

by her decision. Then he asked, "Will ten o'clock be okay?"

"Make it eleven. Isabelle would have left for work by then."

"All right. I'll see you tomorrow around eleven. Goodbye, Jaclyn."

"Goodbye."

She held the phone in her hand long after the call had disconnected. She sat there a moment and recalled everything that had transpired between her and Lucien beginning yesterday in his office. Then she thought about their morning at breakfast and the day they'd spent at the park. When she'd closed her eyes to get some rest earlier, she had convinced herself the relationship building between her and Lucien was more her imagination than anything else. But now that phone call from him proved otherwise. He wanted to be with her just like she wanted to be with him.

She stood and strolled in bare feet over to the window. It was close to seven yet it hadn't gotten dark yet. Should she have turned down his invitation? She knew deep down there was no way she could have done that. Wanting to be with Lucien and his wanting to be with her was a fantasy she refused to deny, no matter the risks. And as ludicrous as it sounded, she intended to enjoy the fantasy as long as it lasted.

But she had to be careful that Isabelle didn't find out. She didn't want to place her roommate and best friend in a comprising position by covering up for her. So the less Isabelle knew, the better off she was.

Just like Jaclyn had felt it was her duty to report

Terrence's drug use to her superiors because he was breaking a hospital policy, she didn't want to place Isabelle in a position of having to do the same. The non-fraternization policy was in place whether she liked it or not. And for her and Lucien to see each other in spite of it meant they were clearly breaking hospital rules and regulations.

She told herself they would have these two days and no more. But as she walked back to the bed and slid under the covers she had a feeling those two days were just the beginning.

Chapter 7

"Okay, Jac-O, what's the reason for that silly grin on your face?"

Jaclyn resisted the temptation to burst out laughing. She had been trying so hard not to let her excitement show but couldn't help it. The last thing she needed was for Isabelle to start asking questions…like she was doing now. Her best friend was known to weasel anything out of her she wanted to know. "I have no idea what you're talking about."

Isabelle lifted a dubious brow. "Yeah, right. And I guess there's no reason why you're up at the crack of dawn when you don't have to go in to work today, or there's no reason why I heard you humming in the shower earlier."

Isabelle then crossed her arms over her chest and

looked at her pointedly when she added, "And no reason why your car is missing. I noticed it was still at the hospital when you left yesterday which was before me. However, when I got off work at noon your car was still there. How's that?"

Jaclyn swallowed under the intensity of Isabelle's gaze. In as calm a voice as she could muster, she said, "I was tired and got a ride home."

Isabelle nodded slowly, still keeping her gaze on her. "And where did you go? You weren't here when I got home."

Jaclyn took a sip of her coffee. "Why the questions?"

"Why the secrecy? Are you seeing someone behind my back?" Isabelle asked in a voice laced with humor.

Jaclyn wasn't sure what gave her away. It could have been that she didn't answer quick enough to suit Isabelle or that she had a blush of guilt on her face. Regardless, Isabelle's mouth dropped open and she pointed a finger at her. "You are seeing someone," she exclaimed.

Jaclyn knew she was in hot water. When Isabelle wanted to know something she was like a dog with a bone. She wouldn't let up until she got her fill.

"Don't you think you're getting carried away, Belle?"

"Um, you tell me, Jaclyn. I've never known you to be so secretive about a man. To be quite honest, I've never known you to get serious about a man period."

What Isabelle said was true. "We're taking things one day at a time and until we test the waters to make sure it's going to work for us, I prefer keeping things private."

Isabelle sipped her coffee and then said, "So in other words you're not going to tell me a thing about him."

"No, for now it's best." Like Jaclyn had decided last night, the less her best friend knew the better. "You're just going to have to trust me on this one, Belle. And before you ask, no, he isn't married."

Isabelle shrugged. "Hey, I couldn't stop that possibility from running through my head. But for once I'll mind my own business until you decide to let me in on what's going on."

"Thanks."

"And if you ever need me for anything, let me know. From what you told me you haven't dated much since that guy you broke off with a few years back. Things have changed. Men have changed. They are more of a dog than ever."

"All of them aren't that way, Belle."

"True, but finding a good one these days is like looking for a needle in a haystack. So I hope you know what you're doing."

She hoped she knew what she was doing as well. But all it took was the memory of their time together yesterday to convince her that although she might be doing the wrong thing, it was for the right reason…if that made any sense.

Jaclyn glanced over at Isabelle who was studying her over the rim of her coffee cup. It took all her willpower not to squirm under her best friend's scrutiny. "There is something I might need your help with, Belle."

Isabelle placed her cup down. "What is it?"

"I'm going out on a date and would like your opinion on an outfit to wear." Jaclyn watched the smile spread over Isabelle's face. She of all people knew that next to practicing medicine Isabelle's other love was clothes. She could hook an outfit together like nobody's business. Even though Jaclyn wasn't a total flop when it came to working an outfit, she knew for this date she needed help. First of all, she'd never been on a boating date.

"Sure I'll help. Where are you going?"

"Sailing on the Chesapeake and possibly dinner later. And…"

Isabelle lifted a brow at her hesitation. "And what?"

"And I might need an overnight outfit. You know, a nice piece of lingerie."

Isabelle covered her face with her hands and literally groaned. "Please don't tell me you're planning to spend the night with this guy."

Jaclyn stood to place her cup in the sink. "Okay, I won't tell you, especially because I haven't decided. Right now we're getting separate rooms. But I want to be prepared just in case."

Isabelle crossed the room to where she was standing and placed her coffee cup down on the counter. "What do you know about this mystery man of yours? Are you sure you want to go that far already? I think we need to talk about this," she said with a scowl on her face. "Sounds to me you're moving too fast, letting your hormones get out of control."

Jaclyn chuckled. "Possibly, but last time I looked at

my driver's license I was twenty-six and you don't look like Hattie Campbell to me. Even if you did favor my mom, I'll tell her the same thing I'm about to tell you. I'm a grown-up."

"Yes, but you know so little about men. You're like a fish out of water. A shark is getting ready to gobble you up."

Jaclyn smiled. "And how do you know I won't be gobbling him first?"

Isabelle stared at her, speechless, for a moment and then she threw her head back and laughed. "Okay, you got me there." She slowly shook her head. "You've become a bad girl right before my eyes."

Jaclyn grinned. "No, I'm finally going after something that I truly want."

"If I didn't know better I'd think you're trying to get rid of me."

Lucien couldn't help but chuckle at the accuracy of his sister's words. She had called right after he'd gotten out of the shower. Last night had been the best sleep he'd gotten in months—at least since the nightmare with Terrence Matthews had begun—and all because he'd known he would be spending the next two days with Jaclyn.

"Not that I'm trying to rush you off the phone, kiddo, but this is my day off and I've made plans."

"What kind of plans? You sound excited."

He pulled the belt through the hoops of his jeans

while cradling the phone against his face with his shoulder. "I'm going sailing on the Chesapeake."

"Mmm, nice. It would be even nicer if you had female companionship on this voyage of yours."

He smiled. Lori was always trying to hook him up with someone. "And what makes you think that I won't have someone with me?"

He heard his sister's sharp intake of breath. She was surprised. "If I'm wrong, then by all means correct me. I'd love for you to do so."

He chuckled. "Yeah, I bet."

"Is it serious?"

"I would love for it to be serious, but already there are roadblocks and they're almost insurmountable."

"Then come up with a plan to get them out of the way. If anyone can do it, you can."

If Lori was here with him, he would have hugged her. She always had more confidence in him than he had in himself. "I hope you're right because failing is not an option for me."

Lucien thought about those words again a short while later as he drove across the Francis Scott Key Bridge on his way to pick up Jaclyn. Failing wasn't an option for him. He wished he could explain what was compelling him to spend the next two days with her and basically risking everything to do so. And he was risking everything. Dr. Dudley could make things pretty damn difficult for him as well as for Jaclyn if word got out about them.

He had called her before leaving home to make sure

her roommate had left for work as scheduled. Jaclyn had answered the phone in an excited voice, one that had stirred emotions inside of him the moment he heard it. He'd known at that moment, short of death, nothing would keep him from spending whatever time he could with her.

Because it was well after the morning rush hour, it took no time at all to reach Jaclyn's home. He pulled his car into the parking space in front of her town house. As he got out of his car he glanced around to make sure the coast was clear. He didn't like the fact that he had to sneak around to see his woman.

His woman?

He stopped walking and inwardly grimaced. Why would he think of her as such? Hell, if you wanted to count yesterday as an official date, that meant this was only their second. She hardly belonged to him. She was merely someone he was intensely attracted to, but they both knew the attraction had a dead end.

Then why are you here? he couldn't help asking himself. *Why are you willing to put your career on the line for an attraction that's a dead end?*

He forced himself to start walking again, refusing to answer that question just yet. He rang her doorbell and felt the rate of his pulse increase when he heard her fiddle with the lock.

And when she stood there after opening the door, he knew the answer to his questions. He knew why he was there the moment he felt heat emitting between them in a connection so electrifying that they could only stand there and stare at each other.

Without saying anything, she took a step back, and drawing in a deep, steadying breath he followed, entering her home.

He filled her doorway and for the life of her, Jaclyn couldn't avert her gaze from his. Nor could she stop the way her pulse was thudding as he stared at her. His eyes were darker than usual and she continued to feel heat—the kind that was giving off an erotic energy. It was an energy she wasn't used to.

She held her breath when he closed the door and slowly covered the distance separating them. He reached out and brushed loose stands of hair back from her face before cupping her chin and tilting her eyes up to his.

It was then that he said, "Good morning, Jaclyn," before slanting his mouth over hers.

She wasn't given the chance to respond when his mouth began mating with hers with a possession she felt in every part of her body. Instead she returned his greeting in a physical way. She wrapped her arms around his neck and drew her body flush with his. This kiss was more powerful, forceful and ignited more passion within her than anything she'd ever experienced, and that included the kisses they'd shared yesterday. She'd thought nothing could top them. But there was something about this one, a confidence or determination or possibly both, that seeped through to her bones.

And just when she thought he had released her mouth

to end it, he took her mouth again, deepening the kiss as a low, guttural hum vibrated in his throat. She heard it. She felt it. And she responded to it, letting him take charge of her tongue while she all but melted into his arms. The way his wet and greedy tongue was sliding against her own made her moan. Desire filled her unlike anything she'd ever felt.

And then he suddenly released her mouth. He continued to hold her while his breathing calmed, regained a semblance of control. So did hers…at least it tried to anyway. She felt his hands gently stroke her back, and all she could do was stand there and rest her head on his shoulder and draw in deep, rapid breaths.

"Around you my control gets blown to hell," he whispered in a low, husky voice close to her ear.

She figured whenever she was able to catch her breath, she would admit her control around him wasn't much better. She lifted her head and her breath got lodged in her throat when she looked into his features. The rays from the sun shining through her living room window hit him dead in the face and made him appear even more devastatingly handsome. She wasn't sure what she liked the most—his sculpted cheekbones, his sensual lips or the tempting darkness of his eyes.

Jaclyn decided she liked all three, but his sensual lips had the ability to make her panties wet just looking at them. And she didn't want to remember how they'd tasted.

"We're getting deeper and deeper into this, aren't we?" he murmured softly against her lips.

Ignoring the shiver that lapped at her nerve endings, she said, "Yes, but don't ask what we can do to stop it because I haven't a clue." Was Isabelle right? Was she moving too fast? Thinking with hormones raging out of control?

After his call inviting her to spend the next two days with him, she hadn't gotten much sleep. Anticipation had overtaken her senses. And when she had opened the door and seen him standing there, it had hit her just how far gone she was where he was concerned. He was right when he'd said they were getting deeper and deeper into it.

"You look nice, Jaclyn. Extremely nice."

His compliment made her smile and she glanced down at herself. "Thank you."

With Isabelle's help they had rummaged through her closet and drawers and found an outfit appropriate for sailing—a pair of white shorts and an aqua blue top. And she had prepared an overnight bag. Once Isabelle had seen her mind was made up about the overnight trip, her roommate had gotten naughty in selecting the outfit to wear this evening and another to sleep in tonight. Although Jaclyn had tried convincing her that sharing a bed with her mystery man wasn't a done deal, Isabelle hadn't wanted to hear it. She'd even put a couple of condoms in the bag, saying it was always best to be prepared.

"Ready?"

"Yes, I just need to grab my overnight bag," she said turning to quickly go to her bedroom.

When she returned he was still standing in the same spot but was glancing around. He looked at her and smiled. "Nice place."

"Thanks."

He then crossed the room to take the bag from her hand. Their fingers touched during the transfer and something inside her rocked. Every sense she possessed was in tune only to him. He met her gaze and she was held captive once again by the darkness of his eyes.

A horn blast from a passing vehicle made her jump, and her lips firmed as she drew in a deep breath. This was crazy. When had an attraction affected her to such a degree? When had it gotten so potent?

"I think we need to get the hell out of here."

She couldn't agree with him more. If they stayed even a second longer there was no telling what they might be tempted to do. "All right."

As they headed toward the door to leave, she had a feeling when she returned in two days her life wouldn't be the same.

"I see you got your car from the hospital," Lucien said as he steered his vehicle toward Annapolis. It was a beautiful day and although the sky appeared filled with dark clouds, the weatherman had indicated there was no rain in the forecast.

"Yes, I got it late yesterday. Because Nurse Tsang saw us leave together, I didn't want to give her any ideas about us. Had my car stayed there all night she would have assumed…"

When she didn't finish what she was about to say, he glanced over at her and asked, "Assumed what?"

He saw the blush staining her features when she said softly, "That we spent the night together."

He didn't say anything for a minute and then, "Yes, I can imagine her assuming that."

For a long moment he tried not to think of the implication of that. Not only would the woman think it, she would tell others of her assumptions. He'd worked at Hopewell long enough to know that for some reason Kayla Tsang had Dr. Dudley's ear when it came to hospital gossip. If Ms. Tsang concentrated more on what she was supposed to do rather than what the hospital personnel were doing, things at Hopewell would run a whole lot better.

"Do you go sailing a lot, Lucien?"

He nodded and smiled while keeping his eyes on the road. It was tempting to look at her, glance down at her pair of gorgeous legs. She looked good in shorts. "Yes, whenever I can get away. The guy who owns the marina where I rent the boat teases me about being his best customer."

"It must be nice getting away from the hospital every now and then," she said softly.

"It is."

He knew as an intern that first year was grueling for them. Most of the time the interns spent the night at the hospital and rarely got to sleep in their own beds at home. Working a double shift was routine. He could remember those days.

"If I don't escape somewhere, I'll find an excuse to drop in to the hospital to check on my patients like I don't think someone else can take care of them besides me." He shrugged his shoulder. "Everyone needs a life outside the hospital to do the things they enjoy. You deserve it. Your patients deserve it. There's nothing worse than a doctor in a bad mood."

"You're a good doctor, Lucien."

He glanced over at her when the car came to a stop at a traffic light. "You think so?"

She chuckled and he liked the sound of her voice. "Yes, and I'm not just saying that because you are my boss. Getting brownie points isn't my style."

"And what is your style, Jaclyn?" he asked, letting his gaze leave her face to trace a path down her body to her legs. He didn't want to think of all the things he would like doing with those legs.

"Mmm, I'd like to think my style is pretty straightforward. I learn not only by observing but by listening as well. I know to ask questions when I don't understand something and won't hesitate to disagree if I truly believe I'm right and someone else is wrong."

She didn't say anything for a moment and then said, "And I don't think there is anything wrong with a person being wrong sometimes. Nobody is perfect. So I guess my style is to always remember that everyone should be treated with respect. When a person comes to the hospital it's because they need us to do what it takes to make them better. We should tend to their needs individually and not collectively and not think we don't need them because we do. I think a dedicated doctor knows that."

Lucien remained quiet as he dwelled on what she'd just said. Her beliefs were going to make her a good doctor, a cut above the others. He had observed certain things about her from the first. In addition to just how good-looking she was, he'd known that she had compassion for those she treated, wasn't quick to diagnose anyone and didn't mind going the extra mile to see to her patients' comfort.

"Sorry, I didn't mean to get on my soapbox," she said apologetically.

"You didn't. I asked a question and you answered it the best way you knew how. I don't have a problem with that."

"Thanks. And what do you see as your style, Lucien?" she then asked him.

He thought about her question for a moment. "I don't think you need to be a drill sergeant to get the best out of anyone, so I don't use that approach with the interns, as you well know. I tell them what is expected and make sure they deliver. I don't bully and neither do I beg. All the interns are well aware of why they're here and what it takes to cut the mustard. Some will make it, while others, like Terrence Matthews, will fail."

He hated bringing up the man, but whether he wanted him to be, he was there right in their faces. He knew the Matthewses were out for blood, mainly his because he was the one who'd fired Terrence. The one good thing was that he had evidence on his side. And for the time being Dr. Dudley. Faced with such evidence his boss couldn't do anything but back him with the firing.

Lucien decided to change the subject. "So how did you meet Isabelle Morales? The two of you seem to be pretty close friends."

"We are. We met years ago at one of those medical student seminars while in college. She was attending University of Florida Medical School and I was at Johns Hopkins. We kept in touch and were ecstatic to discover we'd both landed slots at Hopewell. Her main concern was housing and luckily I had that taken care of. She's a lot of fun as a roommate."

He heard the soft sigh escaping from her lips after she paused briefly and added, "And in case you're wondering but not asking, the answer is no. She doesn't know you're the person I'm spending time with over the next two days."

She chuckled. "Of course Isabelle wouldn't be Isabelle if she wasn't curious. Especially when she knows I haven't dated anyone seriously since we've become friends. But she does respect my privacy."

A part of him should have felt relieved about that, but for some reason it didn't head his list of concerns.

"What about your friendship with Dr. Bradshaw?"

He knew why she was asking. "I haven't mentioned anything to Thomas about spending time with you."

Being confined with her in the car made him very much aware of her scent. It was a sweet yet arousing fragrance that was getting next to him. "So for now this is between only us, Jaclyn."

She nodded. "And I prefer it that way."

His hands tightened on the steering wheel. A part of him should have felt relieved that that was her attitude, but that was not the case. She was a woman any man would be proud to be seen with, but as long as she was his intern there was no way that would be happening. Why was he willing to be with her any way he could, even if it meant behind closed doors?

As he continued the drive to Annapolis, that question weighed heavily on his mind.

When they arrived at their destination it didn't take Lucien long to rent a boat. Jaclyn could tell from the friendly exchange of conversation between him and the manager of the marina that Lucien was a frequent customer like he'd said.

While the two men conversed she glanced around and took in the beauty of her surroundings. She had been so busy at the hospital with so little free time to spare that she hadn't gotten around to checking out all the beautiful places around Alexandria.

The sun was shining brightly overhead in this part of Maryland. It was the perfect day for activities on land or on water and she looked forward to going sailing.

Her lips were still throbbing from the kiss she'd shared with Lucien earlier. Each time she would try to convince herself that maybe Isabelle was right and things might be moving too fast, he would do or say something to make her think that everything was moving at the right pace.

She enjoyed everything about Lucien. He was a great conversationalist and a gentleman at heart. And although she was fully aware of the degree of his desire, she was in no way frightened by it. For her to have fallen in love with him so quickly and easily spoke volumes. But then, according to her parents, things had been that way for them.

"Ready?"

She glanced over at Lucien. He was holding the basket filled with lunches they had grabbed from a restaurant near one of the piers. She didn't have to inhale deeply to appreciate the aroma of fried chicken, reminding her it was past lunchtime and she hadn't eaten anything since that morning. "Yes, I'm ready."

Together they walked on the pier to the boat they would be using. It was definitely a beauty. And it was huge. She glanced over at Lucien. "It's bigger than I thought it would be."

He chuckled. "Relax, I'm a capable captain."

She smiled. "That might be true, but I'll probably fail as your mate. I know nothing about sailing."

"Then I'll look forward to teaching you a few things."

He made good on those words when less than an hour later he not only proved what a great captain he was by his handling of the sailboat, but also just how patient he was when he showed her how to assist him. When he had shown her how to put the life jacket on correctly, she had given him what she hoped was her most appreciative smile, while fighting all the sensations rumbling in her stomach.

And when he had glanced down at her to make sure the jacket was just how he wanted it, she had glanced back up and met his gaze. She had actually felt the heat in every part of her body. Even with all the sexual tension surrounding them she was glad she was spending time with him and couldn't help wondering what tonight would bring.

He had placed her overnight bag in the trunk of the car next to his and it had looked natural for them to be side by side. Ever since then, she couldn't stop anticipating their time together later.

"Daydreaming isn't allowed."

His words interrupted her thoughts and she glanced over at him and chuckled. He was sitting down operating the tiller and keeping the sailboat from sailing directly into the wind. Like her, he was wearing a pair of white shorts and he had a pullover jersey sporting the name of his favorite NFL team.

"Sorry. It's such a beautiful day, I can't help it," she said.

"Then maybe I need to give you something else to do."

She lifted a brow. "Something like what?"

"Like bringing that lunch basket over here. I think it's time for us to eat. I'm starving. What about you?"

Jaclyn was starving as well, so she didn't waste any time grabbing the basket. Taking the tablecloth out of the hamper, she spread it over the small table and emptied the contents of the carrier—a container of fried chicken, pickles, bags of chips and a bottle of wine.

She tried ignoring the shivers of pleasure that raced up and down her spine when she sat beside him. When he inched closer to her, leaned over and placed a kiss on her lips, she couldn't help the goose bumps that formed on her arm.

"I doubt anything in that basket," he said in a low husky voice, reaching up and pushing a lock of hair from her face, "will taste as good as you do."

She wished he hadn't said that. She'd been kissed before, but no man had ever said such a thing to her. She swallowed deeply noting her breathing pattern had changed. And she and Lucien were sitting so close that she could feel his muscles tensing.

She nervously licked her bottom lip and asked, "You think so?"

The smile he gave her could wet a woman's panties. "Baby, I know so."

Jaclyn smiled. "Are you always this complimentary?"

"No, but I always speak the truth."

He was good for a woman's ego and she enjoyed having him around. He was definitely a keeper. "I think we should try tasting something more filling."

He chuckled and leaned back. "Okay, then, woman. Feed me."

Sharing lunch with him was fun. While they ate what she thought was the best fried chicken she'd ever eaten and sipped wine, they talked about anything and everything other than work.

He told her more about his life in Jamaica and some

of the pranks he and his sister had pulled on their cousins. She could tell by the sound of his voice that he missed seeing his grandmother and looked forward to the trip he'd planned for the holidays.

She was enjoying being with him and getting to know the man her heart had already claimed as hers. After a while she noticed they had fallen into silence. As she glanced over at him, she realized he'd been staring at her. "Is something wrong, Lucien?"

He shook his head slowly. "No, I think everything is just right. Things couldn't be more perfect at the moment."

A smile touched her lips. She felt the same way.

Chapter 8

Jaclyn's breath caught when Lucien brought his car to a stop in front of the most beautiful bed and breakfast she'd ever seen. The hour drive from Annapolis to the Eastern Shore had definitely been well worth it. Nestled on a hundred and twenty acres, Wades Point Inn was huge and spacious and provided a scenic and picturesque view of both the Chesapeake Bay and the Eastern Bay.

"So what do you think?"

She glanced over at Lucien and figured she dared not tell him what she thought. They would be here only one night, but already she could imagine all the things they could do together in such a romantic setting. She could envision their seeing the sun rise and set from their room and could picture their holding hands while exploring the nearby quaint, historical towns of

St. Michaels and Easton. And she could definitely see their sharing a glass of wine tonight while watching the boats go by on the bay.

She drew in a deep breath knowing what those thoughts meant. He had left the decision regarding their sleeping arrangements to her and she had made it. They would definitely be sharing a room tonight. She glanced over at him. "I think this place was meant for us, Lucien. It was meant for us to be here. Together."

She knew he had purposely taken them far away from Alexandria and she appreciated his doing so. No matter how the future unfolded for them, she was convinced that this was their time to be together.

His smile was priceless and she knew he'd gotten the meaning of her words. She saw the simmer of heat already forming in his gaze at the thought of what tonight could possibly hold for them. But she wasn't surprised by his next question. "Are you sure, Jaclyn?"

She knew why he was asking. If they carried through with their plans there would be no turning back. Each was making a leap into forbidden territory, regardless of what tomorrow would bring. They were concentrating on only today. Temptation teamed with anticipation and rippled all through her when she said, "Yes, I'm sure, Lucien."

Lucien studied Jaclyn carefully when the receptionist at the front desk handed over their room key. He was looking for any sign that she had changed her mind and didn't want to share a room with him after all. But he didn't see any. What he did see was a woman, a very desirable woman, with a made-up mind.

"Ready to go up?" he asked softly.

She looked over at him and smiled and at that moment he felt like the luckiest man on earth. And when it came right down to it, he was probably also the horniest. Just being with her was making sexual urges hit him from just about every angle.

"Yes, I'm ready."

They had left their overnight bags with the bellman, so he was free to tuck her hand firmly in his as they headed for the elevator. Anticipation lapped at his heels with every step he took. Being with her had basically turned his world on its ear. She had decided that they would share a room tonight. But even if she had asked for her own room, he still would have appreciated this time they were spending together. He knew at that moment, although he wanted her with a passion that he felt to his gut, there was more between them than just sex. A part of him knew it even though he didn't fully understand it.

He was still pondering what was there about her that made him risk everything just to be with her. What had made being with her the ultimate surrender more than a supreme sacrifice was the woman whose hand was firmly tucked in his. The woman who in just two days had opened his eyes to things they had been closed to for years. Besides work there was play and what made it enjoyable was the person you were with.

They stepped into the elevator alone and automatically she turned to face him. It seemed the most natural thing to do when he pulled her closer to him, wrapped his arms around her waist and lowered his mouth to hers.

Her lips parted the moment his touched hers and in the back of his mind there were imaginary fireworks exploding all around them. He delved deeper in her mouth and couldn't help the groan that slipped past his throat. Red-hot sensations rushed through his bloodstream as his mouth continued to not only explore hers but claim it.

The elevator came to a stop so suddenly that it almost jerked them apart, and her sigh of disappointment equaled his moan of frustration. They stared at each other, fully aware that their desire for each other had escalated out of control. Stripping her naked the moment they got to their room seemed like a good idea about now. But it wasn't what he wanted. It wasn't what she deserved. He hadn't brought her here just to jump her bones. Their time together had more meaning than that. Although he would be the first to admit he was getting used to kissing her, getting used to tasting her. Kissing a woman had taken on a whole new meaning. And he didn't want to recall just how she felt in his arms. How her body had automatically curved into his. How soft she felt and just how good she smelled.

He shoved his hands into the pockets of his shorts and walked beside her as they exited the elevator. There was no way he could touch her now. Doing so would be suicide. They needed to make plans to get out of their room rather quickly or they wouldn't be going out tonight.

"The lady at the front desk mentioned something about a concert in the square tonight," he said.

The older woman had explained to them that in the historical town of St. Michaels tonight was jazz night, and suggested they check out the concert that would be followed with a magnificent fireworks display. It had sounded like something he wanted to see and do…until he had kissed her. Now all he wanted to do was get her in that room and kiss her some more.

"Yes, that would be nice," she replied.

He smiled, thinking that she didn't seem too excited about it. "Or if you'd like we can take a stroll around the grounds and then call it an early night," he suggested.

He watched the smile that touched her lips and at the same time temptation pricked up his spine. Hell, forget about the stroll. It would suit him just fine if when they got to their room they didn't come out until checkout time tomorrow. But he knew he couldn't let that happen. He had to remember that as much as he wanted her, it was more than just sex between them.

"Okay, then, we'll take a stroll around the place before dinner," she said.

He expelled a huge breath. He was still reeling from the kiss they'd shared in the elevator, and when they finally reached their room and he inserted the key and opened the door, he had a feeling he was in big trouble.

It should have been relatively simple, Jaclyn thought. She could have turned on the television and watched the news until the bellman delivered their luggage. And Lucien could have moved around the room and checked out the menu on the desk, counted the number of hangers in the closet or studied the design of the bedspread. But that was not the case. As soon as the door closed behind them, she was pulled into a pair of strong, masculine arms.

The second his mouth touched hers she knew they were finishing what they had started in the elevator. A wave of longing washed over her and she felt any control she might have had come tumbling down. The depth of passion that overtook her wreaked havoc on her senses and opened floodgates of emotions she'd kept at bay for eighteen months.

His mouth went still on hers when there was a knock at the door. Then he gave one final sensuous lick of his tongue around her mouth before breaking off the kiss and taking a step back. He frowned at the door, and when he spoke his voice was laden with frustration. "Who is it?"

"Bellman with your luggage, sir."

He glanced over at her. The look in his eyes pretty much made her suspect that he would tell the man to go away and pull her back into his arms. She figured she needed to intercede. "We need our clothes, Lucien," she said, reasoning with him.

"No, we don't."

She laughed. A part of her knew he was serious. "Behave." She immediately moved to the door when she saw he would not.

The bellman entered. As soon as he deposited the bags on the bed Lucien gave him a tip and the guy wasted no time leaving. She had a feeling the man had known he had interrupted something.

Lucien inclined his head toward the door and gave her an innocent smile. "Was it something I said?"

She chuckled. "Your look gave you away, Dr. De Winter."

He slowly crossed the room to her. He placed his hands in his pockets as if he needed them there or else he would reach out and touch her. "And how do I look, Dr. Campbell?"

For some reason she loved it when he referred to her as such. It made her feel like his equal in the professional realm of things. She paused a moment as if to study him. *You look like a man any woman would want.* Those were the words on the tip of her tongue, but she wouldn't utter them. They were thoughts she preferred keeping to herself for now.

Instead she said, "Like a man with a plan."

His brow rose and he frowned slightly as he seemed to study her features. "Do you think the only reason I asked you to come here with me was to seduce you?"

Without missing a beat, she reached out and placed her arms around his neck. "If that *was* the reason I'm not complaining."

She knew that they had pretty much crossed the line when they'd kissed at the park yesterday. And now they were about to spend two days together. She knew what was happening between them, so why did it seem as if he was stalling now?

"I know what this is costing us, Lucien," she said quietly.

He searched her features. "Do you?"

She looked him squarely in the eye and said, "Yes, but I'm willing to take what I can. Whatever you offer."

"Why? Why are you so accommodating to me? I see the other male doctors and the interns and how they look at you, how they check you out. Unlike me they have been free to make their interest known. I know a couple have asked you out, yet you've turned them down. I overheard their disappointed whispers when you did so. But you didn't hesitate to go out with me. Why me and not them?"

She shrugged. "I could say I get a thrill coming on to my boss."

"You could but you won't."

Jaclyn glanced down at the floor. He was right. She wouldn't. Nor would she tell him the real reason. The truth. That she had fallen in love with him the first day they'd met. He would probably find the whole concept of love at first sight ludicrous.

"I like mature guys," she heard herself say, knowing he was waiting for her response. "I like a guy who knows where he's going. A guy who is respected. A guy with whom I know where I stand. I like a guy who I believe won't lead me on. A guy who will give it to me straight."

She dropped her arms from around his neck. Now was the time to tell him more so he could understand. "The last guy I was seriously involved with I dated for almost two years. I thought I knew him. Then a group of his buddies decided to tour England. He had finished law school and it was going to be the last chance he got before he went to work at some law firm or another."

When she paused, longer than she planned to, he asked, "What happened?"

She held his gaze. "He returned at the end of the summer as planned, but…"

"Why did I know there was going to be a but somewhere?"

She smiled slightly. "Mainly because you're perceptive."

She tossed her hair from her face and said, "But he returned just long enough to tell me he was going back to England for a while. He had met someone and he was going to get her and bring her to the States."

"He dropped you?" Lucien asked in an astonished voice.

"Like a hot potato."

"For another woman?" he asked as if the thought of such a thing happening was above his level of comprehension. She saw the way his jaw tightened as if what Danny had done was an insult to him as well as to her.

"Yes, but I got over it and him soon enough." There was no need to tell him that in a way she'd been relieved because she'd realized soon afterward that she hadn't truly loved him anyway.

"Now I only live for the moment," she said, as if she preferred something casual to a committed relationship, which was so far from the truth. But because she knew they could never have such a relationship, she wasn't bothered by the little white lie she was telling.

"So," she said, placing her hands on his broad shoulders. "You know my position. What's yours?"

She stole a look at him from underneath her lashes, saw the heated gaze staring at her. Then in a low, seductive voice he said, "I have several positions, Jaclyn. And I plan to show you all of them. Starting now."

He then lowered his mouth to hers.

Chapter 9

Lucien slanted his mouth possessively over Jaclyn's as desire swept through him. He told himself to slow down, not be greedy but to savor not only the moment but also the woman. However, the deeper he took the kiss, the more he wanted her, the more the need to make love to her became as elemental as breathing.

Her lips were softer, more delicious than anything he'd ever tasted. And as he continued to kiss her he detected it again, in the recesses of her mouth—her unique flavor, a potency he tasted, absorbed and was convinced he was addicted to.

Lucien traced every inch of her mouth with the tip of his tongue before using that tongue to tangle with hers. Sensation after torrid sensation swamped his body. He hadn't wanted to go this far this quickly. He had wanted them to take a stroll around the property, to appreciate their surroundings, to enjoy the bay. But it seemed all those things would be placed on the back burner as they enjoyed each other.

He deepened the kiss while his hands slid up and down her back in leisurely strokes, and he shifted his stance to bring her closer to his hard, masculine frame. She was soft to his hard, but from her kiss he could tell she was just as ravenous as he was. Just as overtaken with desire so arousing that he felt it in his bones.

He tried to draw on the strength he truly didn't have to end the kiss here and now. But the only thing he could do was let his mouth cling to hers and not let go. He'd known he was a goner the moment he had arrived at her house and seen her in those white shorts and blue top. She'd looked more than just cute in the outfit. She'd looked tantalizing with a capital *T.*

There wasn't anything indecent about the way she looked, but all her lush curves had sent blood rushing through his veins, had ignited sensations he'd tried reining under control but couldn't. The only reason he finally released her mouth was because they both needed to breathe.

But that didn't stop his tongue from sensuously licking the sides of her mouth or playfully tasting the bow of her lips as she drew in sharp intakes of breath. There was just something about her mouth—the shape, taste and texture—that could render him mind-bogglingly delirious with need.

And if that wasn't bad enough, he had eased his hand beneath her shirt to roam up and down her back, stroke the softness of her skin. She was wearing a bra without a back opening which meant the clasp was in the front. The thought of freeing her breasts from the bra had heat flowing all through him and sensations tugging low in his gut.

He pulled his hands from beneath her shirt and went for her hair. From the first day he'd seen her he had wondered how it would feel to run his fingers through it. Now he reveled in the silky feel of her brown tresses.

He took her mouth again. Never had he made love to a woman's mouth the way he was doing hers. It was as if he was paying homage to it. And Jaclyn's mouth deserved the honor. She had lips made for kissing and a mouth made for tasting, and he was doing both.

He had known the more he kissed her the weaker to resist her he would become. But the last thing he had expected was this raw hunger, this intense desire that he felt in every part of his body. There was no organ spared, no sensation missed or muscle neglected. All were working simultaneously to give him the Jaclyn Campbell effect. He was getting it in large doses and had no control of what was happening to him at that moment.

"Lucien," she groaned his name, slowly pulling her mouth away and looking up at him.

His gaze snagged hers and the degree of desire he saw embedded in the dark depths almost took his breath away, almost brought him to his knees. He fought back both reactions as he swept her off her feet and into his arms. Moving toward the bed, he thought of the words he could possibly say to make her know just how he felt. He was good with a stethoscope, but when it came to expressing himself where a woman was concerned, he was at a loss for words. Never had he been so overwhelmed.

He gently placed her on the bed, but that was where his tenderness ended. He began undressing her with a need so fierce that he sent her clothes flying everywhere. His intent was to strip her naked. And he wasn't wasting any time doing so.

He paused and raked his gaze over every inch of her bared flesh. Each part of her was so tempting that he had to force his hand to remain by his side, hold his tongue hostage inside his mouth and shift his body to ease the pressure of his erection straining against the zipper of his shorts.

His gaze then zeroed in on her mouth, a mouth that had been thoroughly kissed by him and that tempted him to do so again. His eyes moved up to hers and held her gaze, watched the magnitude of emotions that flickered in their depths.

"You are simply beautiful," he said in a soft, unsteady voice, one filled to the brim with need of the most intense kind. The smile that appeared at that moment on her lips made his gut clench.

"I think you're beautiful as well," she said, letting her gaze roam all over him.

He chuckled. Because he was still fully clothed she didn't really see much skin, but she would and he hoped she thought the same thing when she did. He slowly skirted around the bed to sit in the wingback chair to remove his shoes and socks, not taking his eyes off her.

He saw she was paying attention to everything he did, taking it all in.

After tucking his socks into his shoes and placing them aside, he stood and went to the belt on his shorts and slid it through the loop. Placing the belt aside he pulled his shirt over his head and tossed it away.

His glanced over at her when he heard her sharp intake of breath as she stared at his bare chest. Moments later he eased both his briefs and walking shorts past his thighs and down his legs and the look that flared in her eyes sent red-hot sensations sweeping through him.

He knew at that moment their lovemaking would not only be intense, but it would also be special. The entire room oozed with sexual chemistry. When he picked up his shorts to get a condom packet from his wallet, he had a strong feeling they wouldn't be leaving their room anytime soon.

Jaclyn fought to regulate her breathing as she stared across the room at the man who had the body of an Adonis and wore the most beautiful smile she'd ever seen. Even when a nagging voice inside her mind was saying she should really question being here with him and that maybe things were moving way too fast, she couldn't help the heated desire that seemed to overtake her senses.

She would never forget the first day she'd met him, when he had walked into the auditorium and introduced himself to all twenty interns. She'd heard the feminine whispers that had wafted through the room. Like all the other women she had been checking him out, but unlike them, she saw beyond a handsome face and a well-built body.

When he started to speak, his words momentarily weren't the focus of her attention. She concentrated on the man as a strange phenomenon took place and it was just as her mother had said it would be. She'd discovered that day that love at first sight, as crazy as it sounded, was as true as true could be for her.

The strange thing was that she had known nothing about him other than his name and the fact that during the period of her internship at Hopewell he would technically be her boss. But a part of her had known something else. It had known love in a way she'd never had with Danny. Stranger still was that Lucien had had no idea what she'd been thinking. He hadn't had a clue.

But now he was here. They both were. Totally naked and about to connect in an intimate way. She watched while he encased his manhood with a condom and she couldn't help but lean back on her haunches in the middle of the bed and take it all in, not quite believing the size of him. *And I'm supposed to handle that?*

From somewhere she was suddenly entrenched with confidence that she could and she would. Maybe it was the way he was looking at her watching him. Or maybe it was the fantasy of him tucked away in the back of her mind. Whatever the reason, her body began tingling all over, causing a delicious ache to start throbbing at her center. And when he slowly began moving his naked body toward her, she could only look at him and be totally consumed by him.

He came to a stop at the edge of the bed and said in a deep, husky tone, "I want you."

Okay, so it wasn't the L word, but she would take it. And the meaning, spoken with such profoundness made her tremble. "You're shivering," he said.

She released a deep sigh while thinking that wasn't all she was. She felt as if she was a heated mass of desire and all for one man. Before she could respond to his observation, he reached out and pulled her into his arms.

More than anything, Lucien thought, this was what he wanted. This was what would often make him toss and turn, and keep him up late at night. Thoughts of sharing a bed with Jaclyn, of kissing her this way, of participating in racy foreplay before their bodies joined in lovemaking. His fantasies had been so profound that he would wake up in cold sweat.

Now he was about to experience the real thing.

Her taste was luscious on his lips and while his tongue toyed endlessly and hungrily with hers, he wanted more and tilted her head back to get it. The low moan that escaped her throat when he deepened the kiss made his heart beat that much faster, and caused goose bumps to form on his arms.

His hands smoothed over her back before moving lower to clutch twin cheeks in his hands while easing her on her back. He broke off the kiss long enough to say, "I love kissing you."

The words tumbled from his throat easily and he knew he hadn't experienced anything quite like what he was sharing with her. When he had her flat on her back, he began tasting her from her lips to her breasts. The twin globes were high, firm, and the nipples were dark and inviting and he couldn't resist the temptation to taste them.

He heard her deep sigh and felt her clutch the back of his head to hold his mouth in place when he began sucking earnestly on a nipple. Her scent conveyed her readiness, but he wanted to taste her all over and he slowly left her breasts to move his mouth lower to her stomach.

He was consumed with a hot hunger, a deep desire to lick her all over, taste her and absorb every inch of her into his mouth and the scent of her into his nostrils. Wanting to know just how ready she was for him, he lowered his hand to the wet spot between her legs, slipping his fingers between the damp womanly folds. His body began shivering knowing just how much she wanted him and how her body had prepared to have him.

Desire, as potent as anything he'd ever felt before, rushed through his body as he lowered his mouth, kissing a path downward. When he reached his destination and his tongue entered her, the quivering of her thighs sent a tidal wave of sensations through him.

Never had he enjoyed loving a woman this way more. *This* woman. And he took his time to savor her as well as to bring her pleasure. When she moaned he deepened the intimate kiss, determined that she partake of the dose of rapture overtaking him. And when she called out his name after an orgasm took control of her body, he locked his mouth to her, determined to feast on her to the max.

Moments later when he finally pulled his mouth away, he sat back on his haunches to stare down at her. She wore pleasure well. Satisfaction was carved into her features and she seemed to inhale an air of bliss with every intake of her breath. She held his gaze and he knew from this moment that when he brought her home tomorrow that would not, could not, be the end of things for them. If he'd ever thought that this could be a two-day affair and that when it was over he would return to his senses, he was totally wrong.

"You're ready for me, sweetheart?" he asked, feeling the deep throb of his erection overtake his senses.

Jaclyn could only lie there while toe curling sensations oozed from her body, leaving her feeling bone tired and weak. But she wasn't too weak to respond to what he'd asked. Because although she had just experienced one whopper of an orgasm, all she had to do was read the look in his eyes to know there were more where that one came from and he intended for her to enjoy every single one of them.

"Yes, I'm ready."

A smile curved his lips. Evidently he liked her response. Then he slowly began easing toward her, and her heart began beating more furiously with every inch he took toward her, his warm breath getter closer and closer to her lips. Anticipation was eating away at her, renewing her desire and kicking her hormones into overdrive once again.

And then he was there, touching his lips to hers. No

matter how often they kissed she would always look forward to mingling her tongue with his, eagerly, hungrily, willingly. And when he covered her body with his, she felt the heat of him from shoulder to thigh, especially from his center. It was almost burning her alive.

She felt him fit right between her open legs. The intensity of his kiss deepened and suddenly he thrust inside of her as he held tightly to her hips so she would take him fully. Pleasure ripped through her the moment their bodies connected, and then he began moving in and out while she arched her body to meet his every stroke.

She'd made out with Danny many times, but until today she hadn't known how it felt to be so in tune to a man. The more he thrust, the more she wanted him. His strokes deepened, and so did her need for him.

Finally, she couldn't take any more, couldn't handle the expert precision of his lovemaking another moment. Sensations slammed into her, pushing her over the edge. She broke her mouth from his to scream out his name.

There was not a single disillusionment in how she felt. Every bone in her body felt pulverized, every cell energized, and she knew that no matter what the risks of having a relationship with him might be, it was all worth it. Here, in his arms, was where she belonged.

Lucien soothed Jaclyn's hair back from her face as she slept. She looked beautiful awake or sleeping. He couldn't help but think about what they'd shared moments ago. Never had making love to a woman meant so much. Never had he gotten just as much as he'd given.

He had wanted her badly and she'd given him just what he'd wanted.

He momentarily closed his eyes, just to decipher what kind of future the two of them could have if they continued on this path. And the answer wasn't one he was ready to accept just yet. She was a woman any man would be proud to be seen with. A woman a man should cherish and not sneak around with. She deserved better than that.

He opened his eyes and gazed around the room. They weren't supposed to be here together like this. They were taking a huge risk doing so. But the sexual chemistry, the need and the desire had been too keen, too overpowering. They hadn't been able to resist such temptation.

"Lucien?"

He glanced down at her. Although the room was dark, he could see her gaze. He held it. "Yes?"

She reached up and touched his cheek, traced a line around his lips with her fingertip. "Any regrets?" she asked in a soft whisper.

"None," he whispered back quickly. "It was everything that I imagined it would be. Even more so."

And he meant it. When he'd slid into her body and her inner muscles had clamped on to him, pulled everything he had to give out of him, he had willingly surrendered his all.

He studied her features while breathing in her scent. It was a fragrance he doubted he would be able to forget. "What about you?"

He watched as she drew in her breath slowly before saying, "I wish…"

When she paused, he lifted his brow. "And what do you wish, Jaclyn?"

Her gaze connected with his. "I wished we didn't ever have to leave here."

He wasn't sure if she meant the bed or the inn. Regardless, he was still feeling her. "I wish we didn't have to leave, either."

Beyond the door were things he wasn't ready to deal with. Realities he preferred not to face. He much preferred being here, in this room, in this bed, with her.

But he knew that was impossible. They had a life beyond that door. In another day they would return to their jobs. And it was a job he rather liked doing and he knew for her it was the same. They were who they were. They had simply met at the wrong time.

When he'd left Jamaica many years ago his life plan had been set. From a child he had always known two things: he would one day make a life for himself in America and he would be a doctor. He had worked hard, finished top in his class and he'd played by the rules, refusing to break any.

Until now.

He wanted his job and he also wanted her. He wanted it all, but life decreed that wasn't possible and they both knew it. And it was something he wasn't ready to talk about right now. He just wanted to hold her in his arms and relish the memories.

Moments later he heard her stomach growl and couldn't help smiling.

"Sorry," she said apologetically.

He shook his head. "I'm the one who should be apologizing. We missed dinner. I'll call and have something brought up to us."

"Thanks."

"And I still want to take that stroll tonight. I hear the grounds of the inn are beautiful at night."

"And I'd love to see it…but at some other time." And then she pulled his head down to hers. When she slid her tongue inside his mouth, he moaned deep in his throat and deepened the kiss.

And just like that, she had stoked his desires once again.

Jaclyn opened her eyes to the sunlight shining through the window. She heard Lucien moving around in the bathroom and shifted to lie on her back and gaze up at the ceiling.

It didn't take much to remember last night. It had started with Lucien's mouth on hers and things had moved quickly from there. When it came to kissing, he was a master, but then it was her opinion he was a master lovemaker as well. His strokes and his thrusts had been precise and had aroused her to a point of no return. Never had she been made to feel like that before. In the end they had both lost control. They had both gotten what they wanted. At that moment she didn't want to think about the fact that yesterday and today were all they would have.

"You look beautiful in the morning."

She glanced across the room. He was standing in the

bathroom doorway, shirtless, with a pair of jeans hanging low on his hips. The man epitomized sex appeal.

She sat up in bed and smiled. "And you don't look bad yourself, Doc."

He chuckled as he began slowly moving toward her in what she thought was one sexy stroll. He sat on the edge of the bed and pulled her into his arms and she was ready for the kiss she knew was coming.

Moments later when their lips parted, she could only moan in protest.

"Hey, I need to feed you breakfast," he said, joking.

She shook her head. "No, you don't. We ate dinner late last night, remember?"

And they had. They had made love again before they'd finally ordered dinner delivered to their room. After eating they had gone out on the balcony to watch the fireworks over the bay. The way the prism of color had burst across the water, lighting up the skies, had been nothing short of spectacular. They had slipped into thick terry cloth robes, compliments of the inn, and Lucien had stood with his arms around her waist. She had leaned back into him and had felt like she was the most cherished person on earth. When the fireworks had ended, they had returned to their room, stripped and made love again.

"I still want to go for a stroll around the inn, Jaclyn."

She rolled her eyes. "You're back to that again?"

He chuckled. "You're going to thank me."

She blushed, knowing exactly what he meant. Her body was sore and he knew it. If they remained in their hotel room all day, the soreness would only increase. "Okay, we'll go walking."

Surprisingly it didn't take long for them to get dressed once they got out of the shower a while later. She'd known for them to take a shower together was a mistake as soon as he'd suggested it. But like everything else with him, she'd been tempted and the weakling in her had given in to it.

They enjoyed breakfast on the huge screened-in porch and then they walked around the inn, hand-in-hand, taking in the various sights and sounds. The inn was magnificent, the lawns well kept and the trees and shrubbery neatly trimmed.

Checkout time was at noon, but instead of driving directly back to Alexandria, they had decided to stop along the way and enjoy lunch in the quaint historical town of Evans. After they ate, they walked around the town, and they fell into silence, each one seemingly caught in their own thoughts.

"You're quiet," she said softly.

He glanced over at her and a smile touched his lips. "I was thinking how much I've enjoyed my time with you."

"And I've enjoyed these stolen moments with you as well," she replied.

"Stolen moments…" He seemed to test the words on his lips.

"Yes. Tomorrow we will be back in the real world."

"At the hospital?"

"Yes." They kept walking and then he stopped and turned to her, reached out and tenderly stroked a thumb across her cheek. "And what if I said I still wanted to see you away from the hospital?"

She met his gaze. "Then I would say you would be asking for trouble. You would be taking chances neither of us needs."

He didn't say anything for a while and momentarily broke eye contact with her to glance over the bay. When he returned his gaze to her, he said, "Can you look at me, Jaclyn, and say all you wanted was yesterday and today, and that our time together meant nothing but an affair to you?"

She drew in a slow breath and shook her head. Jaclyn knew her true feelings for him, knew there was no way she could say that. Although the past two days might not have been a turning point for him, it definitely had been for her. She loved him more now than before.

"No, but it doesn't matter what we might want," she said. "The hospital isn't going to change its policies just for us. It is what it is."

"But if I can come up with a plan, would you continue to see me?"

He was gazing at her with such tenderness and longing in his eyes that she knew what her answer would be. She would risk all to continue to see him. "Yes, I would continue to see you."

He nodded. "That means we will have to keep our secret."

She nervously nibbled on her bottom lip. Isabelle would be asking questions when Jaclyn returned. Her best friend was relentless when she wanted to know something.

"I know how you probably feel and what you're thinking," he said, interrupting her thoughts. "I don't like sneaking around any more than you, but that's how it will have to be to protect our careers at Hopewell, Jaclyn. The only other solution is one I'm not ready to do. I'm not ready to give you up and walk away. I'm not prepared to pretend the last two days, especially last night, didn't happen. No matter the cost. You mean more to me than that and I refuse to treat it like it was some cheap hotel-room affair."

Jaclyn didn't say anything. He'd said she meant something to him. Granted it wasn't what her heart declared he meant to her, but at least it was something.

"Jaclyn?"

"Yes?"

"So we are in agreement to continue what we started here?"

His mouth was set in a grim line and she knew he wasn't overjoyed with his suggestion any more than she was, but for them that was the only way. They had their careers to protect and there was no doubt in either of their minds what would happen if word got out they were involved in an affair.

But then she knew what would happen if they weren't involved in an affair. She would be miserable. "Yes, we are in agreement. I'll continue to see you."

With her words she knew a commitment had been made. And it was one she intended to keep. No matter what.

Chapter 10

"Good morning, Dr. De Winter."

He raised a brow as he passed the nurses' station. Was that a smile on Ms. Tsang's face or was it a smirk? He wasn't sure and he really didn't care. The woman was known to cause trouble and he didn't have the time or the inclination to wonder what she was up to now.

"Morning, Ms. Tsang," he said as he kept walking. His day had started off badly. He had to change a flat tire before he could get to work and then got caught in traffic on the Francis Scott Key Bridge. The only good part of his morning was that sitting idle in traffic had given him the chance to relive moments of the two days he'd spent with Jaclyn.

He had taken her home around six yesterday evening and luckily for him her roommate's car was gone, which meant Isabelle wasn't home. But Jaclyn hadn't invited him in because they hadn't known how soon Dr. Morales would be returning. He'd had to kiss her goodbye in a corner of the doorstep where a huge plant had shielded them from possible prying eyes.

He checked his watch as he rounded the hallway to his office. He was eager to see how the patients from the multicar accident were doing. He hadn't gotten beeped on his days off, which meant no emergency had come up while he was away.

Lucien was about to place his key into the lock of his office door but found it already unlocked. He frowned, wondering who'd been in his office. He opened the door to find Dr. Dudley sitting in one of the chairs. He wondered what would have the chief of staff waiting for him at nine in the morning. Had there been some new development regarding the Matthews lawsuit?

"Dr. Dudley, is anything wrong?" he asked, entering his office and closing the door behind him.

"I think we need to talk, Dr. De Winter," he replied in a gruff tone.

Considering that his morning had gotten off to a bad start anyway, Lucien knew he should not be surprised that something was brewing with his boss. Although he hadn't liked the fact that Lucien had fired Terrence Matthews, Dr. Dudley had been backed in a corner where he had no other choice but to support Lucien in his decision. Lucien hoped like hell that given the pressure the Matthewses were exerting on the hospital by withholding funding that Dr. Dudley wasn't thinking about backing down on the stance the hospital had taken.

Lucien went to his desk and sat down. When Dr.

Dudley didn't say anything, Lucien glanced over at the picture of the older woman framed on his desk. His grandmother. He smiled before turning his attention back to his visitor. "I take it this meeting has something to do with the Matthews lawsuit."

Dr. Dudley crossed his arms over his chest and leaned back in the swivel chair. "No, I'm here for another matter altogether."

"Oh? And what matter is that?" he asked.

"Your behavior with one of your interns."

Lucien's stomach plunged. Keeping a poker face, he searched his mind to recall if at any point during the two days they'd spent together he and Jaclyn had run into anyone who worked at the hospital. When he couldn't, he figured the man didn't know anything but was merely fishing for information.

"And just what is supposed to be my behavior with one of my interns? And what intern are we talking about?" he asked in a remarkably calm voice. He leaned back in his chair, hoping there wasn't anyone who had valid proof of his affair with Jaclyn.

"I understand you and Dr. Campbell were seen leaving the hospital together two days ago and her car was still here late in the afternoon."

He inclined his head, seeing clearly now. He shouldn't have been surprised that Ms. Tsang had run to him with her suspicions, just like he shouldn't be surprised that he was acting on it. A part of him wondered again why Dr. Dudley always followed up on whatever gossip that particular nurse tossed him.

"And my leaving here with Dr. Campbell is supposed

to be a crime?" he countered trying to keep the anger from his voice.

"It is if the two of you are breaking the hospital's nonfraternization policy."

"We're not. Like a number of my interns she'd worked a double, taking care of the injured from that multicar collision. But before we got beeped for the accident, she'd come to see me to discuss the Matthews lawsuit. Rumors were going around and she was afraid somehow she would get connected to it. I felt I needed to assure her that wasn't the case and preferred meeting her off-site."

He paused a moment and then said, "And as far as her car being left here for a long period of time…" *Like it's really anybody's business,* he thought. "I offered to take her home when I saw how tired she was. End of story."

Dr. Dudley didn't say anything for a long moment as he studied Lucien. And then, "I hope for your sake, Dr. De Winter, that's the end of the story. You have a promising future at Hopewell. You came highly recommended by Dr. Benjamin Norris, for heaven's sakes. It would be an injustice for you to risk ruining your career by becoming involved with Jaclyn Campbell. I admit she's a very attractive woman and all, but you need to ask yourself if she's worth it."

Lucien returned the man's stare. He would never admit it to Dudley, but he had asked himself that same question last night when he'd gone to bed and this morning when he'd awaken. The answer had been the same: Yes, she was.

Lucien inhaled deeply. He didn't fully understand what there was about his attraction to Jaclyn that he was willing to risk it all to be with her. But it was a risk for her as well.

Yesterday they had agreed to continue to see each other. It was their secret and he intended to protect it any way he could. Even if it meant lying outright to his boss and taking the position of the victim wrongly accused. The one thing that was genuine was his anger. First at the hospital for having such an outdated policy, and then at Dr. Dudley for believing everything he heard.

Besides, his boss, of all people, should not be calling him out on anything. Although Dudley hadn't been accused of any extramarital affairs, he was known to have a roving eye, and Lucien had caught him checking out Jaclyn more than once.

The thought made his nostrils flare in anger and he leaned forward in his chair. "I appreciate your concern for my career, Dr. Dudley, but like I said, it's the end of the story. Unless you have valid proof of any wrongdoing on either my part or Dr. Campbell's, as far as I'm concerned this conversation is over. Now, if you don't mind, sir, I have rounds to make."

He stood up and walked around his desk, grabbed his lab coat off the rack and slid it on before opening the door and walking out. He didn't have to look over his shoulder to know Dr. Dudley hadn't appreciated his exit.

"If I didn't know better I'd think you were avoiding me," Isabelle whispered to Jaclyn as they sat up in the viewing room watching surgery being performed.

Jaclyn inwardly cringed. Yes, she had avoided Isabelle, which was why she had been pretending sleep when her best friend had come home last night and why she'd left early this morning long before Isabelle had awakened. The last thing she'd needed was her best friend grilling her about anything. Although she figured Isabelle's questions would come sooner or later, she wanted to put them off as long as possible.

"I'm not avoiding you. Was there something you wanted?" she whispered back.

Isabelle glared at her. "Of course there's something I wanted. I want to know how about your rendezvous with your mystery man. How was it?"

Jaclyn glanced around. Although Isabelle had whispered the question, Jaclyn needed to make sure no one had overheard. She knew how much people enjoyed eavesdropping. Something was going on today, although she wasn't certain what. She had been at work half a day already and hadn't run into Lucien anywhere.

When Jaclyn had left home early this morning she had gone first to the gym to work out and had showered and changed. Lucien's car was not in the regular parking spot when she arrived at the hospital which meant he hadn't arrived yet. That was unusual because typically he was at work at seven every morning.

Dr. Bradshaw had needed an intern to assist him with surgery and she had volunteered. The surgery was supposed to last a couple hours and ended up lasting four. She'd heard from one of the other interns that Lucien had already made his rounds and was in some sort of meeting on another floor.

"Jaclyn?"

Jaclyn met her friend's curious stare. "It was nice. I enjoyed myself."

"I bet, but I'm not letting you off the hook that easily. Why are you still being so secretive about him?"

If only you knew, she wanted to say. Instead she said, "It's complicated but I promise once I work things out to my satisfaction you'll be one of the first to know."

Isabelle looked at her strangely for a moment, as if she was a puzzle she needed to put together real quick. Then she smiled. "Okay, I'll wait because I know you wouldn't deliberately put me in misery." Isabelle's features went serious when she added, "But you better give me the scoop as soon as you…"

She stopped talking when her gaze latched onto something or someone beyond Jaclyn's shoulder. Then she smiled and whispered, "Don't look now but Dr. De Winter just came in. I swear that man looks hotter each and every time I see him."

Jaclyn's heart started beating furiously in her chest just knowing Lucien was near and she fought the temptation to glance over her shoulder to look at him. Because her back was to the door, turning around would be a sure indication that he'd been the topic of her and Isabelle's conversation.

"You think he's hot, too, don't you?" Isabelle asked when Jaclyn didn't give a response.

Jaclyn shrugged. "He looks all right."

Isabelle frowned and leaned closer to whisper, "Just all right? Girl, you must be blind. Even wearing a lab coat I can tell he has a nice body."

Jaclyn gnawed her bottom lip to keep from saying Isabelle didn't know the half of it. Not only did Lucien have a nice body, but the man also certainly knew how to use it. It didn't take much for her to recall just what that body had done to hers for the past two days.

She was grateful when Isabelle shifted her concentration from Lucien to the date she'd had the night before. From the sound of it, Thurston Reynolds, an attorney Isabelle had met at Cup O'Java Coffeehouse, a hangout for the hospital staff, was a real cutie.

It didn't take long for the doctors to wrap up surgery, and when she stood to leave her gaze automatically went to Lucien. His gaze met hers and she felt a tingling sensation all the way to her toes. She quickly made her way to the door, but of course Isabelle had to make sure they were seen.

"Hello, Dr. De Winter," Isabelle said.

He nodded in greeting. "Dr. Morales. Dr. Campbell." The expression on his face was serious, more so than it had been the last two days. She searched his gaze for some indication of what was wrong. A part of her knew he was bothered by something because he didn't even smile.

Her gaze lingered on him while Isabelle thanked him for recommending her for the pediatric surgery a few days ago. He didn't even glance over at her. They'd said it was their secret and he was definitely doing his part in keeping things undercover.

As she stood there, the only thing she could think about was that her eyes hadn't played tricks on her for the past two days. Lucien was as handsome as she remembered. And she could pick up his aroma even from where she stood.

Moments later Isabelle finally ended the conversation and they turned to leave. Like before, although she was tempted to do so, she didn't look back.

Lucien stood watching as Jaclyn left the viewing gallery. It had taken all the control he could muster not to say "career be damned" and reach out and pull her into his arms.

He had felt her gaze on him the entire time he'd been engaged in conversation with Dr. Morales. More than once he'd been tempted to glance over at her, but doing so would have been unwise. Perhaps even fatal.

"Hey, you okay?"

He glanced up to see his friend, Dr. Thomas Bradshaw, had entered the room from the other side. "Yeah, I'm fine. What about you? I understand you had a pretty complicated surgery this morning."

"Yes, one of the accident victims took a turn for the worse, and he had to be rushed to surgery before eight this morning. One of your interns assisted and she did a real good job."

Lucien lifted a brow. "Who?"

"Dr. Campbell."

He nodded approvingly. "She's good and catches on easily."

"You're right about that." Dr. Bradshaw checked his watch. "I think I'm going to go and grab lunch. You want me join me?"

"No, they served breakfast at that meeting I attended

this morning. I'm good. Besides, I need to make rounds and check on my patients."

"All right, I'll see you later."

Lucien breathed in deeply as he made his way out of the viewing room and down the hospital corridor. He needed to check on the patients still under his care from the multicar pileup. The surgery he'd just seen involved one of them—a married father of two who was still fighting for his life. The surgery had been a success, but the road to recovery for the man would be a grueling one.

As Lucien continued walking, his thoughts shifted to Jaclyn. He hadn't been able to concentrate on the surgery like he should have because he was thinking about her. In his mind he could imagine his nostrils picking up the scent of sex mingled with the most luscious perfume, namely hers.

Today, even with her hair tied back in a ponytail and wearing very little makeup she looked beautiful. Then there had been those few rebellious curls protesting confinement that had fallen in her face. He had been tempted to take his hand and brush them back like he'd done several times these past two days, but doing such a thing would have been a dead giveaway to anyone watching, especially someone as observant as Dr. Morales.

He'd seen the questioning look in Jaclyn's eyes before she had walked off. She had detected something was wrong with his attitude toward her, especially when he'd barely acknowledged her presence just now. He needed to contact her to let her know they were being watched and needed to remain as neutral toward each other as possible.

As he caught the elevator back up to his floor, he thought about Dr. Dudley. The chief of staff would make things hard on both of them if his suspicions were proven right. So right there and then Lucien vowed he'd do whatever he could to make sure that didn't happen.

Jaclyn sighed and rubbed the back of her neck as she looked at the older woman lying in the hospital bed who was trying to be difficult. Even with the short-age of rooms, Nora Allen had insisted on a private one with the view of the Potomac. She had told anyone and everyone who wanted to hear that the famous country singer Jay Allen was her nephew, using that connection to throw her weight around. And it seemed everyone was jumping to her commands in hope they would at least get a glimpse of the singing legend when he flew in to visit his aunt.

Jaclyn glanced down at the woman's chart again. "Ms. Allen, you are scheduled for surgery in the morn-ing. Therefore, your nurse was instructed to remove the polish from your fingernails."

The older woman, whose features showed signs that she was a Botox recipient many times over, gave her a mutinous look. "There's not that much surgery in the world for which I would deliberately take away any armor of beauty I wear."

"Not even when the intent of the surgery is to save your life?" Jaclyn couldn't help but ask.

The woman's glare deepened. "First of all, I can't see

anything life threatening about removing a tiny little mass from my stomach. In fact, I'm sure there's another way it can be removed without surgery. Can't one of those doctors give me something to drink to shrink it and dissolve it away?"

Jaclyn bit back the response she wanted to give the arrogant woman, whom she'd heard had caused nothing but grief to the staff since being admitted two days ago. That tiny little mass she was referring to had the woman looking nine months pregnant. And from the lab reports, chances were the tumor was cancerous.

"Sorry, Ms. Allen, there's no way around the surgery. It's needed."

"So you say. However, you're nothing but one of those student doctors, so your opinion doesn't mean a thing."

Jaclyn took the insult well. "I understand Dr. Meadows met with you last night."

The woman rolled her eyes. "And I'm supposed to believe that old man who looked like he had one foot in the grave and should have retired from practicing medicine at anyone's hospital ages ago? I think not."

"Is there a problem, Dr. Campbell?"

Jaclyn didn't have to turn around to see to whom the ultra-sexy voice belonged. But she did so anyway because he'd asked her a question. "No, Dr. De Winter, there's no problem. However, Ms. Allen has decided she doesn't want her nail polish removed for her surgery in the morning."

She glanced back over at the woman. To Jaclyn's surprise, the glare that had covered Nora Allen's face all day had disappeared. In its place was a smile filled with blatant feminine interest. Lucien was probably young enough to be the woman's son, yet she was lying there and all but licking her lips.

"You're a doctor?" the woman asked Lucien as if surprised.

He chuckled and walked farther into the room. Jaclyn felt heat emitting from him when he came to stand beside her. "Yes, I am. I'm Dr. De Winter."

"Well, Dr. De Winter, I must say that you're a cutie. Where have you been hiding the past couple of days?" Nora asked, still licking her lips.

Lucien smiled. "I had two days off."

"Did you enjoy yourself?" the woman then asked.

"Yes, very much so."

Jaclyn felt an immediate rush of sensations when his response reminded her of what he'd done those two days. Desire thudded through her with a force that nearly knocked her off balance.

He moved closer to Nora Allen's hospital bed, took the woman's hand in his and gazed down at her fingers. "Nice color of polish, but you do understand why it needs to come off, don't you?"

Jaclyn stood there thinking that even if the woman did know she would make sure Lucien told her again anyway just to hold his attention. She was proven right when the woman said, "I think so, but I want to hear it directly from you, Doctor."

Lucien smiled, and the way his lips curved would have taken any female's breath away, so Jaclyn could understand why Nora Allen was lying there with her gaze glued to Lucien's lips. They were lips that had kissed Jaclyn more times than she could count over the past two days. Lips belonging to a mouth that had given her earth-shattering orgasms when it had licked her feminine core. A day later and aftershocks were still flitting through her system on occasion.

Like now.

Jaclyn shifted her stance to tighten her legs together when she felt a tingling sensation between them. And she breathed in deeply trying to get her heart rate under control. She knew now was not the time or place to recall such thoughts, but when the object of your desire was standing less than five feet away from you, there was no help for it.

Jaclyn saw Lucien try releasing the woman's hand, but she held tight. A part of her couldn't blame the woman too much for wanting to share his touch. Jaclyn could only sigh in appreciation that she'd been able to share a lot more than that.

"The reason the nail polish has to be removed," Lucien was saying as Ms. Allen seemed to hang on his every word, "is because during surgery your surgeon will need to check your fingertips from time to time to determine your blood flow. We don't want to take any chances where you're concerned. I want you to get the best of care."

The woman beamed. "And I appreciate that, Dr. De Winter. I have no problem with the polish coming off now that it has been explained to me."

Jaclyn shook her head. Things had been explained to the woman before, although the deliverer probably hadn't looked as yummy as Lucien. Her gaze moved from Nora Allen to see that Lucien had turned to look at her. Had he said something? "Yes, Dr. De Winter?"

"You can call Nurse Sampson back in to remove the polish from Ms. Allen's fingernails."

He then moved to leave the room. She waited, hoping that he would say something—some parting remark—or at least glance over her way. And when he kept walking out the door without looking back, her heart dropped in disappointment.

A few hours later Jaclyn was at her locker to get her things to leave work for the day. She pulled out her phone to see if she'd gotten a call from her parents or brother. She saw she'd received a text message…from Lucien.

Her heart began beating rapidly as she read his brief but meaningful text:

Meet me at our park at five.

Our park. She glanced down at her watch. That would give her just enough time to go home and change clothes before meeting him at *their* park. Grabbing the items she needed from her locker she closed it back and then quickly headed toward the elevator to leave the building.

Chapter 11

Lucien glanced down at his watch for the umpteenth time. Never had he been so anxious to see someone. Jaclyn's car was not parked in her usual spot when he'd left the hospital to come directly here, so he hoped she was on her way.

He adjusted his car seat to further accommodate his long legs and leaned back to enjoy the view of the Potomac from his vehicle. His day had started off badly and it didn't help matters when he'd walked into his office and found Dr. Dudley sitting there.

The man's accusations had definitely struck a nerve, not because they were true but because they reminded him of his wrongdoing. By right he should be meeting with Jaclyn to advise her they shouldn't see each other again because the stakes were too high. But that was the last thing he wanted. However, she deserved to know this new development. It would be her decision if she wanted them to end things.

He turned his head and saw Jaclyn arriving, pulling into the parking lot and claiming the spot directly in front of him. She killed the engine and then got out of the car, one leg at a time.

Immediately his body went into arousal mode as his gaze roamed over her when she closed her car door. She had taken the time to go home to change. She was wearing a printed skirt and matching blouse with a cute pair of sandals on her feet. He couldn't help his appreciative perusal of her entire outfit. There was something outright charming about it. His gaze then returned to her face. Against skin the color of rich creamy cocoa, her hazel eyes seemed to sparkle when she saw him. Her hair was down and flowing around her shoulders and she was wearing a touch of makeup. He especially liked the clear gloss she'd added to her lips.

He thought she looked absolutely radiant. And seeing her someplace other than Hopewell made an abundance of sensations roll along his nerve endings. When she reached his car, he unlocked the door on the passenger side and he watched her slide in. He drew in a deep breath when she unintentionally flashed a creamy brown thigh.

Then she flashed him a smile. "Hi."

Instead of responding to her greeting, he leaned over and captured her lips. Something he'd wanted to do each and every time he'd seen her earlier today. His pulse accelerated when she began playing hide and seek with his tongue, and then quickly tired of the game and began sucking on his.

They shouldn't be kissing like this. They were in a parked car in a public place, for heaven's sakes. Thanks to him, they were yet again taking chances. Pulling his mouth away, he drew in a deep breath and leaned back in his seat and momentarily closed his eyes. How could a woman be so tempting?

"That was some greeting, Lucien."

He chuckled. "Did you like it?"

"Most definitely."

"I'm glad." He kept smiling as he started the engine and looked over his shoulder and backed out of the parking spot.

"Where are we going?"

He glanced over at her. "Someplace where we can talk."

Earlier he had dismissed the idea of taking her to his place, especially with Dudley's suspicions and Ms. Tsang being the nosy person that she was. He wouldn't put it past the woman to find out where he lived and do a drive-by. But suddenly a part of him was willing to risk it. He wanted her in his home. Besides, even if Tsang did a drive-by, Jaclyn's car wouldn't be there.

"Sounds serious."

He glanced over at her when he brought the car to a stop at a traffic light. He hesitated a moment and then said, "Thanks to Ms. Tsang, Dr. Dudley suspects something."

She frowned. "Did she tell him she saw us leave together that morning?"

He nodded slowly. "Yes, and he was in my office first thing this morning to ask me about it."

He turned his attention back to the road. However, he didn't miss the nervous gnawing of her bottom lip. "We need to make decisions." He was sure he didn't need to tell her what about.

Because they were already in Georgetown, it didn't take them long to reach his home. When he parked out front, he couldn't miss the smile that touched Jaclyn's face. "You live here?"

"Yes."

"Your house is beautiful. But then I shouldn't be surprised. This is one of oldest sections of D.C. and my favorite."

Lucien was pleased because this was his favorite section of town as well. He loved the tree-lined streets and the row homes that had been renovated in such a way as to retain their historical significance. "Thanks. Hold tight. I'll get the door for you."

He got out and jogged to the other side to open her door. He glanced around. Because of his hours at the hospital he didn't know a lot of his neighbors and vice versa. In a way he liked the privacy. However, every once in a while he would get an invitation to join the neighborhood potluck night at someone's home. He had yet to show up for one of those.

Lucien opened the door for her and she brushed against him when she adjusted the straps of her purse on her shoulder. The fragrance that drifted from her was arousing, reminding him of the scent of her that he'd carried with him since the time they'd spent together.

They walked side by side up his walkway and inside his house. Luckily for him, today had been one of his neat days. The last thing he'd want was for her to think he was a slob.

"Your home is beautiful, Lucien."

A lazy smile touched his lips. "Thanks, but you've told me that already."

She smiled as she turned around to face him. "Yes, but at the time I was talking about the outside. I like the inside as well. Nice furniture."

"Thanks, but I won't take credit for it. When my sister sold me the place, she left everything behind. She had a new job and wanted a new beginning." There was no need to tell her that Lori's heart had gotten broken here and that she needed to leave and start fresh elsewhere, or that even after three years she hadn't returned once.

"Would you like something to drink?" he asked her.

"No, I'm fine. But you're right. We need to talk, although I'm pretty sure you've made up your mind about things."

He lifted a brow. "You think so?"

"Yes."

He absently picked up a large seashell off an end table. He could remember the very day he'd found it on the beach in Jamaica. He'd been fishing when he'd stumbled across it. Later that day he'd received word he'd been accepted to attend college in America on a full scholarship. After that he'd considered the seashell his lucky charm and it had been with him ever since.

He placed the seashell back down to glance over at her. "And what do you think is my decision?"

"To end things between us. You've decided the last thing you really want is to risk your career at Hopewell to become involved with me."

He didn't say anything for a moment, thinking that ending things between them *would* spare both of them any unnecessary risks. But no matter what she thought, there was no way he could do that. There was no way he could turn his back on what he saw as a developing relationship between them. No matter the risks.

He still wasn't sure what this thing between them was, why was there such intensity and why was he willing to risk everything for an unknown. He just knew he had to. "So you think those are my thoughts," he said quietly. "What are yours?"

He watched her, studied her features. And then he skimmed a glance down her body and felt heat simmer through him. *Keep focus, De Winter,* he admonished, returning his gaze back to her face. He saw her nervously gnawing on her bottom lip and was tempted to cross the room to her, pull her into his arms and gnaw on that lip for her. Then he would lick it a few times before capturing it with his. That would be when the real deal would begin.

He'd discovered on those two days they were together that his desire for her was nonstop and all-consuming. At times, like now, it could take his breath away. Since when, he'd been asking himself lately, could a woman leave him breathless? He knew the answer without much thought. Ever since Jaclyn Campbell had come on the scene and been introduced as one of his interns.

And there lay the crux of his problem.

Jaclyn stood there, not only trying to figure out what to say but also how to say it. Bottom line was that she loved him and had from the first. But that wasn't anything she could share with him. This wasn't about love…at least it wasn't with him. It was about desire, need, attraction and yes, of course, sex.

She had accepted that. More than anything she wished they could end up like her parents. But she was realistic enough to know that wouldn't be the case. However, she would risk all to be with him because of the love she had for him even though she didn't expect him to feel the same way. She didn't like seeing him each day and pretending there was no real emotion between them, but it was what it was.

She saw he was waiting for her response. "My thoughts might be a little more complicated," she said honestly.

"And why is that?"

She drew in a deep breath, not surprised he would ask. "You've made me feel things I've never felt before. This attraction between us is almost bigger than life and in a way it's bigger than my common sense. I'm willing to take my chances and any risks right along with it to be with you."

She had deliberately made it seem that what was between them was merely physical, when for her it was a whole lot more. But he didn't have to know that. A girl had her pride.

"Are you sure, Jaclyn?"

"Yes. However, I'd understand if you want to end things," she said, trying not to be distracted by the way he was looking at her from across the room. Her breathing accelerated when he began walking toward her in that sexy stroll that often had all the young single nurses and interns talking.

When he came to a stop in front of her, he reached out and settled his hands at her waist. "This," he said, leaning so close to her that she could feel his breath on her lips, "is what I want. A chance to hold you, kiss you, get to know you, make love to you and claim you as mine. Even if it's behind closed doors. Ending things between us is certainly not what I want. Maybe it's something I should want for both our sakes, but it's not. I'm willing to risk all for this."

And then his mouth captured hers. His tongue mingled with hers and she couldn't help but release all the desire she'd been holding. He'd said he didn't want to end things and this kiss he was giving her let her know he was dead serious. Passion had erupted, sending them both in a tailspin, and she wasn't sure who began taking off whose clothes first.

All she knew was that when he drew back from the kiss, her skirt was in a heap by her feet. Her blouse was unbuttoned and the front clasp of her bra was undone. His belt was out of the loop and his jeans were unzipped. She licked her lips. Had she done that?

Before she could even think about what she had or had not done, she found herself swept off her feet and into his strong arms.

Lucien walked down the hall to his bedroom while telling himself he needed to slow down. He was thinking with the wrong head, the one below his gut and not the one connected to his neck. But at that moment nothing mattered because what he wanted more than anything was to make love to Jaclyn. He needed to feel his manhood ease into her wet warmth. He needed to feel her muscles clamping down on him hard before milking everything out of him. He needed to revel in the thrusts he would make into her body and appreciate the feel of her moving against him, stroke for stroke.

He reached his bedroom in record time. Before placing her in the center of his bed, he glanced down at her and the look he saw in her eyes sent a flash of blazing heat and desire through him. And when she tightened her arms around his neck and drew his mouth down to hers, he knew how it felt to become obsessed with someone.

When she finally broke off the kiss, he sat down on the edge of the bed with her in his arms. "Don't think when you saw me today that I hadn't remembered what we'd shared over the past two days. But I couldn't be certain no one was watching us or listening to our conversation. Dudley's accusations caught me off guard and of course I denied everything. Tsang is all eyes and all ears and we can't give her anything to work with. As much as I wanted to find you today and pull you inside one of those closets with me and get the kiss I've been craving all day, I couldn't. Right now they're just speculating about us. We have to be careful that we don't give them a reason to do more."

Jaclyn nodded slowly. "All right."

Lucien rubbed a hand down his face in frustration. "Even asking you to meet me at the park and bringing you here was taking a big chance. But I needed to see you outside the hospital. Alone. I needed to kiss you, taste you, let you know I remembered our time together because being with you those two days is something I can't and won't forget."

And then he stood and proceeded to finish undressing her. She then watched as he undressed himself as well as put on a condom to keep her protected. He thought it was something totally arousing to see her watch him do it.

He sauntered back over to the bed and reached out to touch her, tracing a path along the sides of her body before letting his fingertips glide over her firm and uplifted breasts. He remembered them well. Could distinctively recall how they tasted on his tongue.

His pulse pounded at the same time his manhood hardened even more. And at that moment, something inside of him that had dimmed when he'd returned her home yesterday flared to life again.

His breath caught at the thought she could do this to him, that she had that much influence. That much power. But then he'd known after their time in Maryland not to underestimate the power of a woman in control. And as far as he was concerned Jaclyn was in control because she constantly dominated his mind as well as his body.

When it came to stroking him into a tizzy of desire, she could do it instantly. Not knowing when they would have another chance to slip away from prying eyes again, he wanted to make this time between them last a while, give them both memories to savor when they were alone, miles apart in their individual beds.

He began tracing a path downward to the center of her and he could tell she was wet for him. A sharp moan escaped her lips the moment he touched her. "You like for me to touch you there, don't you?" he asked huskily, stirring up her sensual scent as he continued to stroke her.

"Yes, I like it," she responded in a voice that sounded strained to his ears.

He smiled. "Do you want me to stop?"

"No, please don't stop," she implored quietly in a sensual plea.

His fingers moved beyond the springy curls to slide a lone finger between her womanly folds. And then he began caressing her there, stroking her while hearing the sharp intake of her breath. He stroked her into deep, heavy passion. He glanced up at her, studied the intensity of her features, heard the moans from deep in her throat.

"Mmm, you okay?" he asked, thinking her arousing scent was getting the best of him. His mouth watered and his manhood throbbed.

When she stared at him through glazed eyes, her pupils were drenched in yearning. "I want you, Lucien."

He decided this time he would let her be in control, do the leading and call the shots. "Then take me, Jaclyn. Any way you want. "

Chapter 12

Any way she wanted.

Lucien's words gave Jaclyn pause. Their gazes held for a long moment as ideas flowed through her head and she liked each and every one of them. She took a moment to study the handsome contours of the face staring at her. Every angle, every sensual plane displayed strength.

Her mother once told her that you could tell a lot about a man not only by the strength of his features, but also the strength of his character. She knew the man looking at her had both.

And she knew something else as well. He was someone she could not only enjoy spending time holding conversations with, but also someone with whom she could indulge her fantasies. There wasn't a single night that she didn't go to bed dreaming about him, basically making love to him in her sleep. Some of those sessions were so brazenly hot that she would wake up in the middle of the night sweating. But now she was here with him. They were both totally naked and completely aroused. And he had offered himself to her—any way she wanted.

She leaned up and slowly slid her hand up his thigh while holding his gaze. "That's a nice offer, Lucien."

"Glad you think so," he said, his voice showing signs that he was getting more aroused by the minute and that her hand touching him was only adding to his torture.

"I do. No man has done that before. You're my first. But then I've never wanted a man with the intensity that I want you," she said honestly.

His breath quickened and she knew why. She had taken hold of his thick erection. She could feel it thickening even more in her hands. "Nice piece of work you have here, Lucien."

He chuckled, at least he tried to, but to Jaclyn's way of thinking his chuckle sounded more like a groan. "Glad you like it."

"I do, and do you know what I wonder about each and every time I watch you remove your pants and free yourself in front of me?"

He groaned again and she responded by stroking him with her fingers. "No, I don't know what you wonder about when I do that," he said, his breath sounding ragged.

She lowered her gaze and watched for a second as her hands continued to grip him, to stroke him slowly, and automatically she licked her lips before returning her gaze to his face. "I wonder how you taste. You know my taste and I think it's such an injustice that I don't know yours. And because I can have you any way I want, I want to have you that way." With that said, she then rolled the condom off his erection.

She pushed him back on the bed and straddled him, leaned down to place a kiss on his lips. When he tried deepening the kiss, she pulled back but returned to use the tip of her tongue to lick him along his jaw, throat and neck. She liked the taste of his skin and knew she would enjoy the taste of another part of him as well.

"Do you plan on torturing me?" he asked, his voice almost a hushed and husky whisper.

"Not intentionally." was her response. "I like to think we'll be sharing the pleasure. I'll make sure you enjoy it when I get what I want."

His eyes, she noted, were simmering in desire, the red-hot kind, and she thought that was good. He had shown her what he could do with his mouth; now it was time they both found out what she could do with hers. She'd never done this before to a man—not even to Danny. Once when she'd mentioned wanting to do it, he'd seemed to have gotten turned off by the very idea and she'd never brought it up again. But it seemed Lucien was just the opposite and she was glad for that.

Her tongue left his chin and began moving lower toward his chest. After placing kisses there it moved on down but stopped long enough to prod around his belly button. She thought he had a cute one. She smiled upon feeling the way his abdominal muscles clenched beneath her mouth.

Her mouth was on the move again, going lower, and she lifted her head slightly when she noted his thick erection was stiff and jutting straight up as if waiting for her tongue's visit. Her breath quickened at the sight of something so beautiful. He was hot and he was ready.

So was she.

She leaned forward and slid him into her mouth, liking the taste of him, and it seemed her mouth automatically stretched to accommodate him. Grabbing hold of his hips she began working her mouth on him and she could tell from the sounds he was making that she was stirring pleasure within him of the most intense kind.

She felt his fingers run through her hair and the feel of his doing so aroused her even more with a wantonness that was new to her. "Jaclyn." He called her name in a voice that was throatier than anything she'd ever heard from him. She thought there was something special in savoring the heat of him this way, tasting all of him—every engorged muscle, every thick vein. When his body jerked and he gripped her hair to pull her mouth away from him, she locked her mouth tighter, refusing to let go.

"Jaclyn!"

He came hard as his body exploded. Just knowing what they were sharing sent sensations flooding through her the same way he was flooding her mouth, and she still did not let go. She wanted this as much as he did. And when he didn't have anything left to give, she slowly loosened her grip on his hips.

It was then that he took over and flipped her on

her back, quickly donned a condom he grabbed off the nightstand and, with his gaze holding hers, he entered her in a hard thrust. He began moving inside of her in sure, rapid strokes with such precision that she cried out.

But he kept on going, shifting various times and in several ways to provide the ultimate penetration. Their gaze met each time and the look that held them together was another kind of arousing factor that was seeping into their bones.

And then their world exploded and they were tossed into a sea of ecstasy that had them clinging to each other for life, for pleasure. Jaclyn's heart began beating too rapidly and she had to take long breaths to get it back in sync.

For long moments they lay beside each other with labored breathing. To say Lucien had pushed her over the edge was an understatement. She glanced over at him and couldn't say anything. There was nothing to say. She had gotten what she wanted.

"You hungry?"

His question reminded her she hadn't taken the time to eat anything before rushing off to meet him. "I guess I have worked up an appetite."

He smiled. "Good. Although I don't think it would be wise for us to go out any place, I know my way around the kitchen and would love to prepare something for you here," he said, caressing the line of her jaw.

"You would do that for me?"

He chuckled. "Haven't you caught on yet, Jaclyn Campbell, that I will do anything for you?"

And knowing the risk they were taking by being together, she couldn't help but believe him.

Lucien glanced across the patio table at Jaclyn. He had enjoyed preparing dinner for her and having her help. At first he'd been kind of leery to accept her offer because he remembered the times he and Nikki had tried doing that same thing and failed miserably due to her competitive nature. She'd taken his suggestions as orders and stated more than once she didn't like being bossed around.

It hadn't been that way with Jaclyn. She had taken his suggestions as suggestions and they had worked well together in the kitchen. He bit into the steak he had grilled outside in his backyard and appreciating his privacy fence more than ever. At least he wasn't looking over his shoulder wondering who was watching them.

"This place is like a beautiful flower garden. It's so peaceful out here, Lucien."

He smiled. "I think of this as my peace zone. Lori planted a lot of the flowers herself. Most of them are common in Jamaica. During winter the harsh cold usually does them in, but in the spring they miraculously come up again. All I do is water them and sometimes I even forget to do that." He chuckled. "Lori's known to call from time to time and remind me."

"She sounds like a nice person."

He smiled. "She is. You'll like her and I know she's going to like you." He leaned back in his chair. "I wished you didn't have to go home tonight." Earlier he had mentioned the possibility of her spending the night, but they both finally agreed doing so would not be a good idea.

"I wish I could stay, too, but it is what it is."

He knew she was right. They had agreed to continue their affair and take the risks. After making love they had redressed and gone into the kitchen to prepare dinner. They had used that time to talk. They knew how they would have to react toward each other at work. They also knew even when they met at their secret hideaways they would need to be careful as well. You never knew who you might run in to.

So they figured getting away together for out-of-town trips would be best. They had enjoyed the time they'd spent together at Wades Point Inn and discussed the possibility of going back again soon.

"I have a trip to Florida coming up. One of those medical conventions," he said, missing her already. But then maybe it would be good to put distance between them for a week. It was going to be hard to see her each day at work and not let anyone know they were involved. He didn't like the thought of their sneaking around, but there was nothing they could do about it.

"When do you have to leave?" she asked him.

"A couple of weeks." He paused for a moment and then said, "I know things are going to be crazy for us, Jaclyn, but I believe that no matter what, we're going to make it work." *And then what, De Winter? What can you offer her other than more clandestine meetings? More behind-closed-door affairs? Secrets kept hidden? Lies to people you and she cared about?*

"I believe that as well, Lucien."

She didn't say anything else as she continued to eat her food and he couldn't help wondering what she was thinking and how she was feeling. She had agreed to continue their affair and the selfish person in him should have been glad. But the part of him who knew she deserved better than sneaking around with him felt bad about it. And the last thing he wanted was for her to think or even consider the possibility that he was taking advantage of her. Because he wasn't. But would others who knew the situation see it that way? He knew for a fact his sister would not. She was a romantic at heart and would want to read more into his and Jaclyn's relationship than what was there. That was one of the main reasons he hadn't told Lori anything about Jaclyn.

"You're not eating. You're picking at your food."

Lucien glanced up. "I was just thinking."

"If it's on my behalf, please don't."

He wondered if she was a mind reader. "Why not?"

"We've talked. Made decisions. And we know what we want to do and need to do. I'm fine with it."

"But—"

"Please, Lucien," she interrupted by saying. "No buts. Buts can begin leading in regrets and regrets then become doubts, qualms and misgivings. And I don't want that."

He stared at her and she stared at him. "You're sure?" he asked her for the second time that night.

"I'm positive."

They changed the subject to talk about other things. He told her more about his life in Jamaica and she told him about her life in Oakland. When he updated her on the Matthews lawsuit she shared with him her own brother's bout with drugs and subsequent rehabilitation and how he was doing fine now and happily married.

"So you think there's hope for Terrence?" he asked her after taking a sip of his wine. Dusk had settled and he'd already lit the decorative lanterns to light up his backyard. They were sitting on his screened-in patio which was keeping out uninvited mosquitoes. It was a beautiful night and he was enjoying it with a beautiful woman.

"Yes, but first he and his family have to admit he has a problem."

Hours later after she had finished helping him clean up the kitchen, she glanced down at her watch. "It's late and although I left Isabelle a note, she's going to worry. I need to leave now."

He walked over to her. "All right." But neither of them made an effort to move. They just stood there. Then within seconds they were kissing like there would be no tomorrow and he knew at that moment he couldn't fight this. And when he swept her into his arms and headed once again toward the bedroom, he knew from the way she was returning his kiss that she couldn't fight it either.

And at this point in time, he didn't want to.

Chapter 13

"If you happen to be on Corridor C tomorrow, please check on Mrs. Canady. She's such a sweetheart," Isabelle said of one of her patients as she downed the last of her coffee before grabbing the handle of her luggage.

It was Isabelle's parents' thirtieth anniversary and she was returning home to the Bronx for a huge celebration and wouldn't return until late Sunday. "I'm going to miss you," Jaclyn said, walking her to the door.

"Yeah, right. I don't believe you as long as you're keeping the identity of your mystery man hidden from me."

Jaclyn gave her best friend a wry smile. "You're not going to let up with that, are you?"

"No, not until I meet him. You claim he isn't married, so there has to be a reason you're keeping him well hidden."

Moments later Jaclyn stood at the window and watched Isabelle pull off, thinking about her best friend's parting words. She hadn't given a response because she wasn't sure what response she could give.

It had been a little more than three weeks since she had first gone to Lucien's house that day where they'd made love and then later made dinner. Even now she could remember how it felt sitting across from him on his screened patio while jazz music played in the background and lanterns cast a dim light on all the beautiful flowers in his backyard.

For her it had been the most romantic evening and even now she could still get goose bumps remembering how they'd made love again before she'd left. That night had been the beginning of many more to come.

During the day at Hopewell, although it was becoming more and more difficult, they played their parts as Dr. Lucien De Winter and Dr. Jaclyn Campbell—both very much aware they were being watched by Nurse Tsang. On more than one occasion she had caught Dr. Dudley eyeing them suspiciously as well. They made sure they didn't take the same days off and on those occasions when they did, they made sure they left town, far away from accusing eyes.

Although Isabelle teased her sometimes about her "mystery man," for the most part Isabelle didn't ask questions anymore and Jaclyn appreciated her for that. Still, it was getting harder and harder to keep her secret from her best friend; especially those times when Jaclyn would smile for no reason after spending time with him.

And they were spending time together. Sometimes

they would travel all the way to Baltimore to meet and stay for the night. One weekend they had gone to New York. Right before he'd left town they'd returned to Wades Point Inn, which had become their favorite secret hideaway. The more time they spent together, the more they wanted to be together. It was getting harder and harder for her when they were apart.

She moved away from the window and headed toward the laundry room to sort out her clothes. Lucien had left a week ago to attend that medical conference in Florida and would be returning sometime in the morning. Although he had called her every night, she still missed him. She couldn't help but do so because they'd begun spending more and more time together.

Jaclyn knew he was still bothered about the situation they were in and the secrets they were keeping from the people they cared about. But they had agreed they had too much at stake to trust anyone right now.

Jaclyn had put in her first load of clothes when she heard the doorbell. Wondering who it could be, she made her way to her front door. She figured after doing her laundry she would curl up with a good book.

She glanced out the peephole in the door and her breath caught. It was Lucien. She quickly opened the door. "Lucien? When did you get back? What are you doing here?"

Instead of giving her answers, he reached out and pulled her into his arms.

How could any man miss the taste of a woman so much? Lucien wondered as he pressed his mouth to hers and then as soon as she parted her lips, he slid his tongue inside her mouth. He needed to kiss her with a desperation he wasn't aware that he could experience.

And just as he knew she would, she reciprocated and her tongue began dueling with his as a rush of heated desire skirted through his system. He'd known to expect that as well. He was convinced he was incapable of ever getting enough of kissing her, of tasting her, of making love to her.

He automatically deepened the kiss and pulled her closer to him. Not only did he need to kiss her, but he also needed to feel her all over. His hands ran down her back before cupping her backside. She felt so damn good in his arms and a part of him wished he would be able to touch her like this forever.

Her heart was beating fast and he felt it, pressed against his own that was pounding just as furiously. Her taste could spur him to do some of the most outrageous things and it wouldn't take much to push him over the edge. He wouldn't hesitate to make love to her right where they stood.

But now he just wanted to take his time to savor what he'd missed. And he definitely missed this, the feel of her soft and compliant lips beneath his that were goading him with an urgency that he felt all the way to his toes, stirring up sensations inside of him. She could ignite his passion in a way it had never been lit before he'd met her.

Moments later when he finally pulled his mouth away, he heard her sigh of both disappointment and pleasure and it mirrored his own. He gently cupped her chin in his hand so their gazes could meet, and he whispered in a deep, husky voice, "I missed you."

He wasn't sure just how much he'd missed her until now. When she had opened the door it seemed as if a weight had been lifted off his shoulders. Although they had talked every night while he'd been away, it hadn't been the same. Even during the day when they were at the hospital, pretending to be no more than associates, at least he would see her. But for an entire week he had to endure the hardship of not seeing her at all. And now that he was here, he didn't want to let her go.

"And I missed you, too, Lucien."

His breath shuddered on her words. The last couple weeks with her had been the best he'd ever shared with a woman. Because they were limited as to where they could go and just what they could do, a lot of their time—in and out of bed—was spent talking. So he felt that he'd gotten to know her pretty well. And everything he had assumed about her in the beginning was true. Besides being devastatingly beautiful, she was smart, kind, a great conversationalist, confident, sharp, gifted…

He could have gone on and on as he looked at her, standing before him with lips that still glistened from his kiss. Last time they were together he'd placed passion marks all over her body. He doubted they were still there, which meant it was time for him to place a few new ones on her.

"Lucien, you took a chance coming here."

Her words reclaimed his attention. "You told me last

night that Isabelle would be leaving around noon. It took all I had to wait until then to get over here."

"But—but what about your car parked outside?"

A smile curved his lips. "I didn't drive here. I caught a cab a few blocks from my house. And I had the cabbie put me off one street over from here."

She shook her head as if she was utterly amazed. "You went through all that trouble?"

He reached out to snag her around the waist and brought her closer to him. "Yes, I missed you and had to see you. I hadn't planned on coming home until tomorrow, but when we finished early, I got an early flight back."

He paused a moment and then asked, "Isabelle did leave, right?"

She chuckled. "If she hadn't, you'd be in a world of trouble. What were you thinking?" she admonished.

"I told you. I was thinking of seeing you and being with you." And then he leaned over and captured her lips.

When Jaclyn tried to ease out of bed in the wee hours of the next morning, an arm reached out and grabbed her around the waist. Lucien then shifted on his back. "Where do you think you're going?"

She chuckled as she glanced over at him thinking the shadow on his chin made him appear sexier. "Some of us have to go to work today. Go back to sleep."

He reached out and grabbed the back of her neck to bring her face close to his for a kiss. He finally released her mouth and smiled at her. "You'll come see

me before you leave?" he asked in a deep, husky voice
as he shifted to his side.

"Only if you promise to keep your hands to yourself," she said, trying to regain her equilibrium. His
kisses could do that to her. "If you don't, I'll be late,"
she added.

By the time she had come out of the bathroom after
showering, she saw he had drifted back to sleep. Not
wanting to wake him, she left a note letting him know
she would be home today around six. She was glad she
and Isabelle had stocked the refrigerator that week. She
knew that Lucien would wake up hungry.

Jaclyn knew something was going on the moment
she arrived on her floor at Hopewell. There was a buzz
in the air and several doctors and nurses were in groups
talking. She hoped there wasn't any new negative development in the Matthews lawsuit.

She saw Tamara St. John and quickly walked up to
her. "Hey, what's going on?"

Her fellow intern pulled her off to a private spot. "I
got here an hour ago and the hospital was swarming
with security. It seems someone has hacked into the
hospital's fertility clinic database to get the sperm bank
records."

Jaclyn lifted her brow. "Why would someone do
something like that?"

Tamara shrugged. "Who knows? But I understand
the real concern is that back in the day a number of the
med students and interns hard up for money sold their
sperm to the clinic. I guess those guys are now wondering if they will be exposed as some baby's daddy."

A short while later Jaclyn was heading to Corridor C to check on Mrs. Canady like she promised Isabelle when she encountered Ms. Tsang coming out of a patient's room. She hadn't seen the nurse for the past couple of days and she hadn't been missed.

"Ms. Tsang," she greeted in a formal voice.

"Dr. Campbell." The woman paused and then said, "Is Dr. De Winter back from his medical seminar? The patient in C5, Nora Allen, has been asking about him. It seems he made somewhat of an impression on her."

Jaclyn lifted what came across as a nonchalant brow. "Really? And why would you be asking me about Dr. De Winter?"

A smirk appeared on Ms. Tsang. "He's your boss."

"And Dr. Dudley is yours. Do you know where he is twenty-four seven?" Her question actually made the woman blush. Jaclyn found that interesting.

"No, of course not. I just assumed…"

"And what did you assume, Ms. Tsang?" she asked, her annoyance with the woman clearly evident.

"Nothing."

The woman quickly walked off and Jaclyn watched her go while easing out a deep breath. Kayla Tsang was determined to unravel something on her and Lucien, but neither of them intended to give her the chance.

As she kept walking toward Mrs. Canady's room she couldn't help but think about what Tamara had told her. Lucien had been an intern here some years ago. Was he one of those men who had sold their sperm to the fertility clinic? Was there a woman out there who'd had his baby?

Jaclyn felt a sudden jab of jealousy at the very thought and tried to shrug it off but couldn't do so easily. She knew that what he did before he met her was none of her business. In truth, what he did now was no business of hers, either. Her only comfort was that he had labeled theirs an exclusive relationship. Secret but exclusive.

She smiled when she thought how unknowingly Ms. Tsang had come to the truth. Not only did Jaclyn know Lucien's whereabouts, but he'd also been in her bed all night. She didn't want to think about what would happen if Ms. Tsang or anyone else found out about that. She guessed Ms. Allen would just have to pine for Lucien a couple more days because he wouldn't be returning to work until then. She smiled at the thought of what Lucien would be doing on his off days.

"You have such a pretty smile, Dr. Campbell."

She inwardly cringed when she glanced up and saw Dr. Dudley. "Thanks, Dr. Dudley."

She kept walking. There was something about him that made her uneasy. Maybe it was the way he looked at her with lust-filled eyes. And the man was married, for heaven's sakes. Some people, especially men who were evidently going through some sort of midlife crisis, never ceased to amaze her.

Lucien hung up his cell phone after talking to Thomas Bradshaw who'd called to inform him that someone had hacked the fertility database. Thomas was one of the men who'd once donated sperm and like others were concerned the information might get in the wrong hands. Fortunately, Lucien was not worried.

Although a lot of interns had gotten together and gone over to the clinic that day, he hadn't been one of them. The thought of his child out there without his knowing the mother hadn't sat well with him. Possibly because he had thought of his own predicament while growing up without a father in his life.

Thomas was hoping security found the culprit. Lucien was certain most of the men who'd donated sperm wanted to remain anonymous and he hoped that continued to be the case. He didn't want to imagine the purpose of someone obtaining those records.

He walked over to the oven to check what he had cooking. Jaclyn would be surprised when she got home to discover he had dinner already prepared for them. He glanced around thinking he really liked her kitchen. It wasn't as large as his, but he liked how she had things arranged, all within easy reach.

By the time she got home she would have put in at least twelve hours today. He of all people knew how hectic an intern's schedule was, but he worried about her. He glanced up when he heard the key in the door and moved quickly to be there when she opened it.

"Hi."

"Hi, yourself," she said, entering the house and closing the door behind her.

That was all she was given a chance to say when he pulled her into his arms. "Dinner's ready," he said, after releasing her mouth.

She lifted a brow. "You cooked?"

He chuckled. "You asked like you've forgotten that I can."

"No, I was wondering why you did. I figured you'd want to rest. We could have ordered out."

"But I wanted to do that for you. You've put in a long day. Interns' hours are too long."

She grinned. "You're the boss. Change it."

He gazed at her thoughtfully. "I would if I could, believe me. It's hospital policy to cram all your training into two years."

"I understand. I was just teasing," she said, taking her purse straps off her shoulder and placing the bag on the table. "Give me a minute to freshen up and I'll be back. I'm hungry."

Then she said, "Ms. Tsang asked about you."

He frowned. "Any reason she did that?"

"Just her typical nosy self. I think she was hoping that I'd slip up and say something I shouldn't. And Nora Allen in C5 has been asking about you."

"The patient who didn't want her nail polish removed?"

Jaclyn smiled. "Yes, she's the one. She's back in the hospital. I think you made quite an impression on her."

He slowly walked over to her. "And what if I said that you made an impression on me?"

She lifted her mouth to his after saying, "Mmm, that sounds rather nice."

He then lowered his mouth to kiss her.

"As usual this is delicious, Lucien," Jaclyn said as she took another forkful of mashed potatoes. Neither hers nor Isabelle's ever got this fluffy.

"Thanks. Anything interesting going on at Hopewell?"

"Yes, I forgot to mention that someone hacked into the fertility clinic database. I understand a number of doctors who were interns at the time were donors. They're beginning to freak out at the thought that someone might come after them as their baby's daddy."

She paused and then looked across the table at him curiously. "Anything you want to tell me?" Jaclyn hoped she didn't sound like a jealous woman, although she inwardly felt like one now.

He shook his head. "No, because I wasn't one of those interns. I didn't ever want a child who didn't know I was its father."

Jaclyn released a deep breath of relief. She appreciated how he valued the thought that a child deserved both parents and she knew why he did so. He'd told her that he grew up never knowing his father.

"Earlier you mentioned my hours at Hopewell, so I might as well tell you I found out that all the interns' hours are increasing over the next few weeks."

He frowned. "I didn't approve that."

"Dudley did. And from what I understand it was Nurse Tsang's suggestion. She thinks we have too much of a life and all of us think she needs to get one."

He got up from the table with his plate. "I don't agree with any of you working additional hours," he said with anger in his voice. "You work enough hours already. I intend to let Dudley know how I feel when I return to work in a few days."

"What if he starts wondering why you give a hoot about how many hours an intern works? He might try putting two and two together, Lucien. Thanks to

Nurse Tsang, he already suspects something is going on with us."

His frown deepened. "They can't prove a thing."

Jaclyn got up from the table thinking he was right. They couldn't prove a thing…unless they saw all those passion marks under her scrubs.

"Did I tell you how much I like your bed?" he asked, breaking into her thoughts.

"I figured you did." Last night was the first time he'd slept in her bed and she had slept like a baby knowing he was there. At least she had slept like a baby when he hadn't been making love to her.

"How long will Isabelle be gone?"

"Till Sunday night." She smiled across the table at him. "That means you're free to stay here until then… and especially because you like my bed so much."

He chuckled. "Thanks for the invite. I definitely plan to take you up on it. I want to hang around and pamper you on my days off, assuming an emergency at Hopewell doesn't call me in."

"When you do return to work it's pretend time for us again," she said, trying not to sound as disappointed as she felt.

"Yes, it's back to pretending again."

As she carried her plate over to the sink, she thought that for them the pretense would probably never end.

Chapter 14

"Not so fast," Lucien ordered in a teasing voice.

He couldn't hide his chuckle while watching Jaclyn quickly rip into what had been a nicely wrapped gift. Her lips then spread into a smile and she glanced up at him.

"This is for me?" she asked with awe in her voice when she stared back down at the diamond solitaire necklace.

He laughed. "Who else would it be for? We've been seeing each other for a month today and I wanted to give you something."

She glanced back up at him. "But when did you have time to go shopping for anything?"

He knew why she was asking. Since returning from the medical seminar in Florida two day ago, other than the time he'd caught a cab back to his place to gather a few of his belongings, he'd been camped at her place.

If anyone had the inclination to be nosy and ride by his place, his car was parked out front and a timer would turn his lights on and off at certain times to make it appear he was there. But where he had been was here spending every possible moment with Jaclyn when she wasn't at the hospital.

"I bought it while I was in Florida. There was a jewelry store in the hotel. I saw the necklace in the window one day, liked it and thought it should be worn around your neck."

What he hadn't told her was that it had been his third day there and he'd been thinking of her, missing her like crazy. Talking to her every night hadn't been enough.

"That was so sweet of you," she said softly. "I'll cherish it forever and it will always remind me of you and our time together."

His lips thinned. Why did she make it sound like a parting gift?

"Will you fasten it around my neck?" she asked, too busy taking the necklace out the box to notice the scowl on his face. Maybe that was a good thing because he couldn't explain the reason for it.

Honestly, De Winter, do you really expect her to subject herself to a secret affair forever? It will be just a matter of time before she decides she wants better. She wants more. And rightly so because it will be just what she deserves.

She turned and presented her back to him and tilted her head to the side while pushing her hair out of the way. After fastening the necklace, he couldn't resist kissing her there.

"What are you doing?" she asked over her shoulder.

"Tasting you," he said, leaning down and kissing that spot on her neck again while tugging her back against him.

To balance their bodies he braced his legs apart which only cradled her hips into the confines of the lower part of his body. He sucked in a deep breath when her bottom brushed against his zipper. That was all that was needed to make his erection start throbbing.

"Stay still," he warned, tightening his arms around her.

"Why?"

"Because I said so," he answered. What he didn't tell her was that he liked the feel of his erection nudging her backside. His jeans and her shorts weren't a barrier from the heat they were generating.

"Lucien," she said in that voice that did crazy things to his pulse.

"Yes?"

She turned around in his arms to face him. "I'm going to miss you when you return to your place later."

Her words reminded him that he would have to leave today because Isabelle would be returning tonight. To play it safe he had decided to leave not long after lunch. "I'm going to miss you, too. But you know where I live. And you're welcome over at any time."

After dark. By taxi. In disguise. He then felt anger that those were the only choices he could offer her when she deserved so damn much more. She needed to be involved with someone who could take her places, be seen out in public with her.

"What's wrong, Lucien? Why the frown?"

His gaze lingered on hers a moment before he simply said, "You deserve more."

She chuckled. "More? You don't think this diamond is big enough or something?"

She was trying to make light of the situation and they both knew it. "I'm serious, Jaclyn."

"Yes," she murmured softly. "I know you are and that's what makes you truly special. I told you a month ago today my decision about us, Lucien. Nothing has changed."

His heart began beating hard in his chest. That's where she was wrong. Something had changed, but he wasn't certain what. All he knew was that whenever he would dwell on the state of their relationship he would feel as if he was drowning in guilt. He would feel something else, too. Emotions he couldn't put a name to just yet. Then again, maybe he could and he was just afraid to do so. Those thoughts made him remember the conversation he'd had with Dr. Waverly one night in Florida over a few beers. Dr. Waverly was the new chief of staff over on the E.R.

"Lucien?"

Jaclyn recaptured his attention. "Yes?"

"You've gotten quiet on me," she said softly.

He regarded her for a moment and then said, "Didn't mean to." His lips quirked into a smile. "I guess I'm just going to have to make up for wasted time."

He lowered his head and his body shivered inside and

out the moment their lips touched. And then it was on when he proceeded to kiss her, taking her mouth with searing intensity. He had enjoyed kissing her from the first and now four weeks later that hadn't changed. The power in her kiss could overwhelm his senses, make every cell in his body respond and every muscle in his body quiver.

She was returning his kiss in such a provocative fashion that he felt his erection pressing hard against his zipper. It wouldn't take much to take her here, standing up. Or over there on the sofa, lying down. Or on the kitchen counter kneeling before her while he—

"Ahem."

The loud clearing of someone's throat had them jumping apart. Too late. They turned and found Isabelle standing there with a combination of shock and humor on her face.

And then with a smirky grin on her face, she said, "Mmm, maybe it wasn't a good idea for me to catch a ride and come home early after all."

A hour or so later Jaclyn leaned back against the front door after seeing Lucien out of it to catch a cab. After her surprise appearance, Isabelle had beat a hasty retreat to her bedroom, pulling her luggage behind her, and hadn't been seen or heard from since.

Jaclyn knew her friend was giving herself time to absorb what she'd walked in on and what it all meant. Jaclyn could just imagine what Isabelle was thinking about now. She pushed away from the door deciding now was the time to find out.

The two bedrooms were separated by attached baths, both off halls from the living room in different directions. It was a good setup for privacy. That gave Isabelle her own space while Jaclyn had hers.

She knocked on Isabelle's bedroom door. "Come in."

Jaclyn squared her shoulders, opened the door and stepped in. Isabelle was unpacking and from the looks of things, she'd been shopping while in New York. "I owe you an explanation," she said quietly, not sure where she should begin.

Isabelle glanced over at her but didn't stop unpacking. "No, you don't. What you do is your business. I just hope the two of you realize what can happen if you're caught," she said point blank.

Isabelle then threw a shopping bag on the bed and gazed at her, drawing her in the full scope of her eyes. "For crying out loud, Jaclyn. Your mystery man is Dr. De Winter. He's not only your boss but he's also mine."

"I know. That's why I didn't want to tell you. I didn't want you involved in our deceit. And you would never have found out if you hadn't come home early."

Isabelle lifted a chin and crossed her arms over her chest. "And just how long did the two of you plan to keep it a secret? Until some big executive at Hopewell decides that the nomfraternization policy isn't needed anymore? You and I know that won't happen, so why are you risking it all, Jaclyn?"

Jaclyn breathed in deeply and met her friend's confused gaze as she said, "Because I love him. I know it might sound crazy, but I had fallen in love with him the moment I saw him my first day at Hopewell. Even before he opened his mouth to say a single word."

She could tell by the weird look Isabelle was giving her that her best friend found that hard to believe. "Does he love you?" Isabelle wanted to know.

Jaclyn turned and glanced out the window. She tried to deflect the magnitude of Isabelle's question by thinking that her best friend had a better view out her window than she did.

"Jaclyn, ignoring me won't work. Does he feel the same way about you that you do him?"

Jaclyn turned back to Isabelle. "I'm not sure. He's never said he did, but then I've never told him how I feel, either. Right now we're just enjoying each other's company."

"And is his company—although you can't convince me it's not more than that from the looks of that kiss— worth it? Is it worth being kicked out of your internship program because you want to play doctor, literally?"

"Yes, it's worth it because I believe my love is worth it, regardless of how he feels about me. And now you know. But I'm asking something that I probably don't have a right to do and that is for you to keep our secret as well. Asking you to do so makes you a part of our deceit."

Isabelle waved off her words. "Hey, although I wish your mystery man was someone else, my lips are sealed—you know that. I promise to keep your secret."

Jaclyn drew in a deep, relieved breath. "Thanks, and just so you know, Nurse Tsang suspects something. She saw us leave one morning together and has put a bug in Dr. Dudley's ear. Lucien and I have been careful."

Isabelle frowned. "Miss Thang needs to go somewhere and sit down. That woman has nothing to do with her time other than to go around gossiping. I would love to get something on her so she could see just how it feels." ·

Jaclyn nodded her head. "Stand in line. I don't think there's an intern in our program who wouldn't like to get something on her, especially after she suggested that Dr. Dudley give us more hours."

Jaclyn then told Isabelle about the increase in their work hours starting tomorrow.

"Are they crazy?" Isabelle all but screamed. "We work too many hours now. I didn't know how tired I was until I slept that entire first day at my parents' home. I was totally drained."

Jaclyn knew exactly how she felt. "Well, just be prepared." She turned to leave the room.

"Jaclyn?"

She turned back around. "Yes?"

"I didn't have a clue about you and De Winter. How have the two of you managed to keep it a secret?"

Jaclyn thought about her question as well as what her response would be. Then she said, "Because we wanted to be together and were determined to make it work. It hasn't been easy, trust me."

"I can imagine. I doubt I could pull off something like that."

Jaclyn gave her a warm smile. "Yes, you could if your heart was at stake. And trust me when I say my

heart is so full of love for him that I can't imagine a
time when we won't be together, although such a time
will eventually come. That's why I need to absorb all I
can get now."

She chuckled quietly and added, "Whoever said that
love will make you do foolish things knew exactly what
they were talking about."

Chapter 15

Lucien pretended to be reading a patient's chart when he saw Jaclyn out of the corner of his eye. Anger twitched in his jaw. She, along with all the rest of the interns, had been working extra long hours. They were all tired and he knew it.

He had tried reasoning with Dudley and the man just wouldn't discuss it, saying the interns needed to prove they could handle things under extreme pressure. Lucien had tried to get him to see that an extremely tired intern was just an accident waiting to happen. He could just imagine one of them slipping up and giving a patient the wrong medicine. The thought of that happening gave him the shivers.

He placed the chart in the rack and glanced over at Jaclyn. She was talking to a floor nurse and he could tell by the lines around her eyes that she was tired. She had pulled a sixteen-hour shift yesterday and a twelve-hour one the day before. On top of that he knew she'd been battling flu-like symptoms for a week.

"Is there anything wrong, Dr. De Winter?"

He glanced over at Nurse Tsang. "What makes you think something is wrong?"

She gave him a rueful smile. "Because you're just standing there staring at Dr. Campbell."

Damn! Had he been that obvious? "I'm waiting for her to finish talking with Nurse Atwater. I need to ask her a question about one of her patients," he lied.

"Oh, I see."

Lucien frowned. The woman saw too much. When Nurse Atwater walked off, he began walking toward Jaclyn. They had been busted a couple of weeks ago when Isabelle had walked in on them. According to Jaclyn, her roommate would keep their secret and he was grateful for that. The next time he'd seen Isabelle he had expected her to pull him to the side and read him the riot act for what she saw as a sleazy backdoor affair, but she hadn't. In fact, if he hadn't known for certain the woman had walked in on him and Jaclyn kissing, he would wonder if he'd imagined it. Not only had she not said anything, but she also hadn't acted any differently toward him.

"Dr. Campbell, wait up," he said when he saw Jaclyn about to get in the elevator.

She turned toward him and his heart almost dropped. Not only did she look extremely tired, but it was also evident she wasn't feeling well. Why was she doing this to herself? "Yes, Dr. De Winter?"

"It's obvious, Dr. Campbell, that you aren't feeling well. I think you need to take a few days off."

She blinked. "I can't take time off. I just caught a bug. I'll shake it in a few days."

"I'm not taking any chances, Dr. Campbell," he said in a firm voice. "It's not good for you to be around the patients. I'm sending you home."

She glared at him and lowered her voice. "Really, Lucien, that's not necessary," she whispered.

"I think it is, Doctor. I want you to leave here immediately." He frowned. "And why are you holding your stomach?"

"No reason," she all but snapped before turning to walk away.

Lucien watched her go and when he turned around he saw Kayla Tsang standing at her station staring at him. He then asked her the same question he had asked earlier. "Is something wrong, Ms. Tsang?"

A smirk appeared on her face. "No, Dr. De Winter, there's not anything wrong."

"I can't believe he's sending me home," Jaclyn said angrily to Isabelle as she walked toward the break room to grab a snack out of the vending machine.

"Hey, don't look for any sympathy here," Isabelle was saying. "I told you this morning that I thought you needed to stay home and get some rest."

Jaclyn rolled her eyes. "Why do I need rest?"

"Because you're sick. And I agree with Dr. De Winter, you don't need to be around patients."

Jaclyn glared at her. "Whose side are you on?"

Isabelle smiled. "Yours. When you're well. Otherwise

I'm in with Dr. De Winter. You need to take better care of yourself. I heard you moving around last night with stomach pains. You need to get checked out."

"I'm fine. I'm just experiencing flu-like symptoms."

Isabelle rolled her eyes. "I can't stand a doctor who tries to diagnose their own condition."

"Whatever."

Jaclyn was about to step in the elevator when suddenly she felt dizzy at the same time a sharp pain ripped through her stomach. She heard Isabelle call her name when everything began turning black and she felt herself tumbling to the floor.

Lucien had just left a patient when he got paged. He went to the nearest phone, punched in a couple of numbers and said crisply, "This is Dr. De Winter."

"And this is Dr. Isabelle Morales. Jac…I mean Dr. Campbell…just passed out."

Lucien's heart dropped. He forced himself to stay calm. "Where is she?"

"She wouldn't go down to the E.R. like I suggested, but she did give in and agreed to be seen by a doctor on staff."

He was moving although he wasn't certain which direction he should go. "What floor?"

"The fifth."

"I'm on my way." And not caring who saw him, he all but took off running toward the nearest elevator.

"Acute appendicitis?" Jaclyn said, staring at Dr. Bradshaw like he had two heads. "There must be some mistake. I have the flu."

Dr. Bradshaw shook his head. "Trust me, I know what I'm taking about. You might have flu-like symptoms, but you don't have the flu, Dr. Campbell. You have acute appendicitis and it needs to come out immediately."

"But—"

"No buts. You're a doctor, so you know the dangers of a ruptured appendix."

Jaclyn began nibbling on her bottom lip. Yes, she did know and that's what scared her. Now the shoe was basically on the other foot. Treating patients was one thing, but becoming the patient was another. "I need to think about this."

Dr. Bradshaw glanced up from filling in his chart. "There's nothing to think about. You need the surgery immediately."

Jaclyn opened her mouth to say something, but suddenly the curtain was pushed aside and she literally caught her breath when Lucien walked in. And she could tell from the look on his face he was both angry and worried.

"Jaclyn, are you all right? What happened?" he asked quickly moving toward her and pulling her into his arms.

She went willingly and gazed over his shoulder and met the surprised look in Dr. Bradshaw's gaze. She immediately knew her and Lucien's cover had gotten blown to smithereens. Lucien then touched her chin to bring her gaze back to him and placed a kiss on her lips. "Sweetheart, what happened?"

Before she could say anything, Dr. Bradshaw cleared

his throat. "Hey, you two, remember me?" he asked teasingly. Then he added in that same teasing voice, "And remember the hospital's nonfraternization policy? So if I were you, Lucien, I would shield my reaction to Dr. Campbell's health issue so it won't be apparent what the two of you have been up to."

Lucien glanced over at his close friend. "Go to hell, Thomas."

"Yeah," Dr. Bradshaw said chuckling. "But not until Dr. Campbell is doing better. She needs surgery."

"Surgery?" Lucien echoed.

"Yes," Dr. Bradshaw said. "She has acute appendicitis and her appendix needs to come out immediately. She's being difficult."

Lucien raised a brow. "Difficult in what way?"

Dr. Bradshaw smiled at Jaclyn and ignoring her frown he returned his gaze to Lucien. "When I told her she needed the surgery she said she needed to think about it."

Jaclyn's frown deepened. The two men were conversing like she wasn't there. It was her medical issues they were discussing. "Excuse me, Dr. Bradshaw, but isn't there a privacy law prohibiting discussing a patient's medical situation with a nonfamily member?"

"That was before Lucien kissed you," the man replied seriously, all manner of teasing gone from his voice. "I know Lucien. He's a close friend who loves his job as much as I love mine. And for him to risk that by breaking a hospital policy tells me a lot."

The man paused a moment and added, "And it tells me a lot on your behalf as well, Dr. Campbell, because

I'm sure your career is important to you, too. But the most important issue at the moment is your health. Like I said, you need surgery immediately."

Jaclyn nervously nibbled on her bottom lip and she glanced over at Lucien. Before she could say anything, the curtain was pulled aside once again. Dr. Dudley walked in. He glanced at everyone in the small room before looking back at her. Jaclyn was certain he'd taken note of how close Lucien was standing to her bed.

"I understand one of our interns passed out, Dr. De Winter," he stated in an authoritative voice.

Lucien took a step back. "Yes, and I needed to see how she was doing," he said as if to explain his reason for being there.

Dr. Dudley glanced over to Dr. Bradshaw. "What's the diagnosis?"

"Acute appendicitis. She needs surgery immediately."

Dr. Dudley nodded. "Then let's get it scheduled," he said as if Jaclyn's decision wasn't needed.

He then glanced over at Lucien. "Don't you have a conference call with that attorney they hired to handle the Matthews lawsuit in less than ten minutes, Dr. De Winter?"

Before Lucien could blow their cover, Jaclyn quickly spoke up. "Thanks for dropping by to check on me, Dr. De Winter. I really appreciate it."

Lucien turned to her and she hoped he could read the plea in her gaze. He did. Without saying anything, he nodded and then left the room.

Lucien hung up his phone, grateful the conference call had lasted only ten minutes. And more grateful that the attorney had only a few questions to ask him because his mind hadn't been able to function worth a damn.

He stood and began pacing the room. He knew he needed to pull himself together, but how was he expected to do something like that when the person he cared about, the one woman who had come to mean the world to him, could be in danger?

It didn't take much to remember nine-year-old Brittney Adams whose parents had brought her to the hospital last year, hours too late. Her appendix had ruptured and she had died on the operating table. He had been the one to deliver the news to her parents.

The thought of losing Jaclyn that way made him shiver from the inside out and he didn't have to wonder why he felt that way. He loved her. For a while he'd suspected he had but hadn't wanted to own up to it because he'd known what that meant: choosing the woman he loved over the position he had worked so hard to achieve.

But the choice had been taken out of his hands. It was technically a no-brainer. Jaclyn meant more to him than his career. He wanted her no matter the professional cost. He was tired of their sneaking around for stolen moments to be together. She deserved more. They deserved more.

And a part of him refused to believe she hadn't fallen in love with him, as well. No woman could give herself to a man the way she gave herself to him without love.

He crossed his office to the window and looked out. But it seemed he could have it all thanks to that conversation he'd had with Dr. Waverly back in Florida. The man had been so impressed with the way Lucien had handled the emergency involving the multicar accident that he had told him if Lucien ever wanted to switch departments he'd love for Lucien to come over to E.R. and take the position of head doctor.

Lucien had been thinking seriously about accepting the man's offer. No longer being Jaclyn's boss meant they wouldn't have to sneak around anymore. Without wasting any time he moved back to his desk and picked up the phone to make a call.

"This is Dr. Waverly."

"Yes, Dr. Waverly, this is Dr. De Winter. Is that offer you made in Florida still out there?"

"Most definitely. I'd love to have you as a part of my E.R. team. I've seen you in action. I can't think of anyone else I'd want as my head doctor."

"Thank you and I accept your offer. How soon can we make the change?" Lucien asked. He preferred working with Dr. Waverly than Dr. Dudley. It was time for him to break camp and move on.

"I'll put in the paperwork today. Are there any special requests?" Dr. Waverly chuckled. "Now is the time to make them."

"I have two weeks off around the holidays this year. I promised my grandmother I'd be home in Jamaica for Christmas."

"That's not a problem. I'll approve those days off for you now as part of your lateral-move package."

"Thank you," Lucien said.

"No, I want to thank *you*. And I'm looking forward to working with you."

After he hung up the phone Lucien glanced at his watch. Thomas had texted him earlier to say Jaclyn's surgery was scheduled for three, which gave him ten minutes to get to the surgical floor. He planned to watch from the gallery and hoped and prayed nothing went wrong. He loved her and knew there was no way he could go on without her.

"How is she, Thomas?"

Thomas Bradshaw smiled at Lucien as he exited the O.R. "Hey, man, I know you were watching, but I'll answer anyway." All amusement was removed from his features when he added, "She was lucky. Had we waited any longer her appendix would have ruptured. Passing out was in her favor. She had to have been in tremendous pain and working all those hours didn't help. Her body was extremely exhausted. I'm going to give her a generous amount of recovery time away from here. She needs it."

Thomas then looked at him curiously. "What about your relationship with her? You can't keep taking chances. If Dudley finds out you can kiss your career here goodbye."

Thomas glanced around to make sure they weren't overheard when he added, "Personally, I think although you did the right thing in firing Terrence Matthews, Dudley is holding it against you, anyway. Especially in light of all the problems the Matthewses are causing the hospital. I know how much your career means to you, so I hope you have a plan B."

"I have. I've accepted the position as head doctor of E.R."

Thomas smiled. "Hey, that's wonderful and Dudley won't go up against Waverly, especially when the hospital moved mountains and courted him like the dickens to bring him here. Obtaining someone with the credentials of Waverly is the only stellar thing Dudley has done lately, and he knows it. Trust me, he'd want to keep Waverly happy."

Lucien nodded slowly. "When can I see Jaclyn?"

"In a few. They're wheeling her to recovery now." Thomas paused and then asked quietly, "You love her, don't you?"

Lucien pulled in a deep breath. "Yes, with all my heart. I didn't realize just how much until the thought of losing her became a reality. Then I knew I could no longer sneak around with her. She deserves more. We both do."

Jaclyn slowly opened her eyes while several jumbled images floated through her mind. She was still at the hospital, but she wasn't standing up and moving around; she was the one lying flat on her back in a hospital bed. She was now the patient. With that realization she felt the pain which made her remember why she was there. Acute appendicitis… Surgery…

"You're awake."

She blinked at the sound of the deep, husky voice and shifted her gaze to her side. Lucien was sitting beside her bed. She opened her mouth to speak, to ask what was he doing there. He would blow their cover if he didn't leave. There was no reason he should be sitting at her bedside and holding her hand. What if Dr. Dudley or Nurse Tsang walked in?

"Shh, don't try to talk, sweetheart. Just listen to what I have to say."

He paused a moment and then said quietly, "I love you. I think I've known it for some time but wasn't sure what to do about it, how to go about handling the situation we'd boxed ourselves in with the hospital's nonfraternization policy. But none of that matters now. Your medical issue made me realize it doesn't matter. It's time we live our lives for ourselves and no one else. And I believe you love me, too. Thanks to you there's no way I can think otherwise."

Jaclyn felt the tears spill out of her eyes. Lucien loved her! She couldn't speak, so she moved her lips to say, "I love you, too."

He smiled. "And don't worry about our careers. We'll be able to work things out and have it all."

Jaclyn didn't understand what he meant and wanted to ask him, but she felt sleepy all over again and could barely keep her eyes open.

"Go back to sleep, Jaclyn. You need your rest. I'll still be here when you wake up. I'm not going anywhere."

Jaclyn held his gaze. And looking into his eyes and seeing the love so blatantly shining in them was the last thing she remembered before sleep took over once again.

* * *

Just like he'd promised her, Lucien was still there at her bedside a few hours later when he saw Jaclyn open her eyes. He had gotten off work more than five hours ago but had refused to leave her side. Isabelle had dropped by several times and so had several other interns. No one questioned his reason for being there, although he'd seen some curious glances. He was certain there would be some buzz about it. Both Dr. Dudley and Nurse Tsang had come by, although he doubted it was out of concern and not out of just plain nosiness.

"Welcome back," he said, gazing over at Jaclyn. "Feeling better?"

"Yes."

He was glad she had her voice back although it sounded kind of raspy. "Is there anything you want? Anything I can get you or do to make you more comfortable?"

"Lucien, what are you doing here?"

By asking him that question he wondered if she had remembered their prior conversation. He decided to jog her memory. "I'm here because I love you and I can't imagine being any place else."

He saw the frown settle on her beautiful face and knew she was remembering. Moments later she said, "But what about our careers? I love you too, but—"

"I have it all taken care of. In a few weeks I will become head doctor in E.R."

"You're changing departments?"

"Yes. That means I will no longer be your boss. And as for your remaining under Dudley, he is smart enough not to hassle you because he has no proof of anything between us before today. I'm sure he and Nurse Tsang have put two and two together, but he can't prove anything. And he knows what kind of trouble he can get into if he files any kind of report based on speculation. That means your career is safe as well."

"And you think he will let the matter go just like that?" she asked.

"Knowing Dudley, I doubt it, but he can't and won't try doing anything about it. Dr. Waverly approached me about the position while we were in Florida. Dudley knows the hospital considers Dr. Waverly the golden calf. It took a lot of hard work to get a doctor of his caliber here and Dudley's not going to do anything to piss him off."

"But will you be happy in the E.R.?" she asked and he could tell by her tone that she truly needed to know.

"I'll be happy practicing medicine, sweetheart. But it's really a blessing for us. I couldn't keep you behind closed doors any longer. I wanted to be with you and be seen with you. It would have only been a matter of time before our secret got out and both of us risked losing our careers. This way our careers are safe and we can be in love out in the open."

"And you want that?"

"Yes," he said, and he meant it. He eased closer to her bed. "And there's something else I want."

"What?"

"To marry you. Make you my wife. I love you. Will you marry me, Jaclyn?"

He saw tears form in her eyes and saw the way her

lips trembled. "I fell in love with you, Lucien, that first day I met you, even before you said a single word to me," she said brokenly. "My mom said it would probably be that way for me because it was that way when she met my dad. She said she'd known all along that Danny wasn't the man for me and that I'd know him when I saw him."

A smile touched her lips when she added, "Although I knew you were the man for me, I just wasn't sure I was the woman for you."

He leaned over and placed a kiss on her lips. "You are. I can't imagine living my life without you. You don't know just how scared I was during your surgery. I watched from the gallery while thinking I could lose the most precious person in my life. I would not have been able to go on without you, sweetheart."

"Oh, Lucien," she said, swiping at her tears.

"And I want you to go home with me for Christmas, to meet my grandmother, my sister and all my cousins." He chuckled. "Although I think I need to warn you that I told Lori about us earlier today and she's already making plans to come here to meet you."

He paused and then said, "And if you want we can have a small wedding in Jamaica and another one here in the States. And just so you'd know, I called your parents."

She lifted a surprised brow. "You did?"

"Yes. They needed to know about your surgery and I also told them what you mean to me. I asked your dad's permission to marry you and he gave it."

Jaclyn drew in a deep breath, thinking she doubted

she could love him any more than she did at that very moment. He had worked out everything for them to be together, and that meant all the world to her.

"Thomas said you'll be able to go home tomorrow if you continue to improve. I've talked to Isabelle and she knows you'll be staying with me. Your parents are flying in tomorrow and I have plenty of room for them to stay at my place."

He slid her hand from his and got up and went to lock her hospital room door. He didn't want any interruption while they sealed their marriage agreement. He returned to stand by her bed. "I love you, sweetheart, and when you get better we'll go shopping for a ring."

And then he leaned down and kissed her and he knew for them it would be a new beginning. One filled with plenty of love.

* * * * *

HOPEWELL GENERAL
A PRESCRIPTION FOR PASSION

Book #1
by *New York Times* and *USA TODAY*
bestselling author
BRENDA JACKSON
IN THE DOCTOR'S BED
August 2011

Book #2
by
ANN CHRISTOPHER
THE SURGEON'S SECRET BABY
September 2011

Book #3
by
MAUREEN SMITH
ROMANCING THE M.D.
October 2011

Book #4
by *Essence* bestselling author
JACQUELIN THOMAS
CASE OF DESIRE
November 2011

www.kimanipress.com

KPHGSP

NEW YORK TIMES AND *USA TODAY*
BESTSELLING AUTHOR

BRENDA JACKSON

invites you to discover

BACHELORS
in
DEMAND

Book #1
BACHELOR UNTAMED

Years ago, Ellie's hot summer flirtation with Uriel
ended disastrously. Now, anxious to complete
her great-aunt's unfinished romance novel, she's
determined to get some firsthand experience by
reigniting their affair. But can Ellie convince Uriel
that their no-strings fling could be the real thing?

Book #2
BACHELOR UNLEASHED

They had a hot, fleeting affair Farrah Langley
has never forgotten. Xavier Kane was tender, sexy
and attentive. Getting together with him again is
a fantasy come true. She certainly doesn't expect
the footloose bachelor to change his ways.
But this time around, Xavier wants more....

**On sale now
wherever books are sold.**

www.kimanipress.com

REQUEST YOUR FREE BOOKS!

2 FREE NOVELS
PLUS 2 FREE GIFTS!

KIMANI™ ROMANCE

Love's ultimate destination!